The Plant Healer

A Novel

James Lake

First printing, March 2025
Library of Congress Control Number: *pending*
ISBN 978-1-953136-95-4 Hardback
ISBN 978-1-965784-00-6 Paperback

Cover Design by Kurt Lovelace
Cover Artwork by Pierian Springs Press
Cover type *Bauhaus Dessau* **Alfarn** by Céline Hurka,
Elia Preuss, Flavia Zimbardi,
Hidetaka Yamasaki, and Luca Pellegrini.
Body & Chapter Titles set in **No 9T**
Headers in **Jenson** by Robert Slimbach
Flourishes set in Emigre Foundry **Dalliance**, by Frank Heine
&
Emigre Foundry **ZeitGuys**, by Bob Aufuldish, Eric Donelan.
Typefaces licensed Adobe, Linotype, Emigre, & URW GmbH.

PSPress.Pub
Pierian Springs Press, Inc
30 N Gould St, Ste 25398
Sheridan, Wyoming 82801-6317

This book is dedicated to everyone around the world who cares about the earth.

CONTENTS

 ALSO BY JAMES LAKE | 112

 ABOUT THE AUTHOR | 113

The Plant Healer

"There is something infinitely healing in the repeated refrains of nature—the assurance that dawn comes after night, and spring comes after winter."

RACHEL CARSON
Silent Spring

1

The door to Dr. Chandler's office stood open and he was sitting at his desk, studying a leaf through a magnifying glass, his bifocals perched on the fleshy tip of a rather bulbous nose.

"Good morning, Henry," I said from the doorway, still feeling a little awkward about using his first name. "There was a note in my mailbox saying that you wanted to see me."

"Ah yes," he replied, briefly glancing up at me. "Come on in and have a seat, my boy, and I'll be with you in a minute."

So I did as he asked, choosing the closest of the two brass-studded leather armchairs directly across from him. It was a fairly typical botanist's office. Heavily laden bookshelves. Various collections of dried plants under glass. Even a shiny new microscope for when he got truly serious about analyzing a specimen. And he'd certainly done a lot of that in his nearly forty years here at Fairfield College, the last twelve firmly entrenched as the departmental chair.

"So," he said as he set aside the magnifying glass and leaned back to release a bit of a sigh. He was a portly fellow with thinning brown hair and a florid face, old school in everything from his three-piece tweed suit to the meerschaum pipe that he liked to puff on during faculty meetings. "It's been an oddly tumultuous past couple of weeks, hasn't it?"

That was putting it mildly. The shootings at Kent State had taken place just the Monday before last, leading to so much civil unrest on our quaint little campus that the administration had had no choice but to shut the school down and send all of the students home. And yet, as I was soon to discover, that wasn't at all what Henry had really wanted to talk about.

"Let's just hope," he then went on, "that everything will have calmed down by the start of the fall semester. In the meantime, what I actually called you in to discuss is your first year review, which as I'm sure you remember is written into your contract."

Yep, I was well aware of that all right. It was just the latest on a long list of bureaucratic formalities I'd been forced to endure over the past nine months that made me wonder why in the hell I'd ever accepted this position in the first place. But this certainly wasn't the time for me to complain about that. So I merely gave Henry a slight smile and waited to hear what he had to say.

"All in all your performance has been commendable," he began, opening a manila folder that lay on his neatly organized desk, drawing out a printout of some kind, and giving it a quick review. "Your teaching record is superb. You've made some very important contributions to both the Undergraduate Studies and Curriculum committees. And for the most part your colleagues consider you to be both personable and easy to work with."

And having said that, he set the printout down and gave me what I took to be an oddly foreboding look.

"But?" I ventured tentatively.

And his expression immediately softened. "But there's the matter of your publications," he then said in a sympathetic, even fatherly tone. "I realize that this is your first truly academic appointment, Devin, even though you've recently turned... what is it now, thirty-two?"

"As of just this last month, yes."

He acknowledged that with a shallow nod. "And I also realize that before coming here you led quite the adventurous life, exploring the world in search of new plants that might prove to be beneficial to mankind."

He broke off to remove his glasses and wipe the lenses, leaving a brief silence that merely heightened the suspense of whatever he was about to say next. "And yet," he said, slipping his glasses back on, "you have to keep in mind that Fairfield is a private college, not a state-funded institution, so we depend heavily on alumni donations and endowments to support us financially, and because of that the administration most definitely prefers the faculty to do research of a, shall I say traditional nature? In other words, research that doesn't risk creating the type of controversy that might alienate some of our more conservative donors."

Aha. So that was it. "And because most of my research over this past year has dealt with the psychoactive properties of plants you want me to tone it down just a little. Is that what you're trying to tell me?"

He released a heavy sigh. "Think of your grandfather, Devin. Think of his legacy."

Believe me, I did. In fact I thought about both nearly every single day, for it was only due to my grandfather and his legacy that I was even here in central Ohio. Not only was he the very first chair of Fairfield's Botany Department, but he'd actually founded the department as well. So when the Dean of Arts and Sciences contacted me a little over a year before to see if I might be interested in applying for the newly established David Douglass Endowed Professorship, I ultimately decided that I owed it to my grandfather to at least throw my hat into the ring, so to speak. Granted, taking the job would mean a radical change of lifestyle, but I'd recently entered my thirties and had been a vagabond traipsing all over this good green earth for the better part of the past eight years, so I thought that maybe it was high time for me to settle down for a while. At the moment, however, I wasn't so sure that I'd made the right choice.

"So what you're saying," I told Henry, "is that the powers that be here at Fairfield would prefer me to do work that's a little more conventional. Or to put it another way, work that's more socially acceptable according to their narrow standards."

"Now don't be so quick to take offense, Devin," he cautioned. "I've known you ever since you were a little boy, you know, and you've always been one to challenge the system, even in your youth. It's just that a college is not only a seat of higher knowledge, it's also a financial entity. And we can't risk our financial stability pursuing the kind of research that might possibly cause us to lose much-needed funding. So if you have even the faintest desire to stay on here after your appointment ends next year, it would be to your benefit to toe the line. I'm sorry to have to say that, but it's the unavoidable reality of your present situation."

"I appreciate that advice," I told him, "and I'll definitely take it under consideration. Although given the fact that my grandfather was your mentor throughout most of your career, I can't help but ask where you personally stand on the matter."

He thought that over for a moment, his mind drifting back in time, and then eased into a hint of a smile. "Well, in spite of the fact that he was a traditionalist academically, your grandfather was also somewhat of a romantic, and in the final years of his life he often spoke of you and your adventures in what I would have to say was a rather envious manner. He was proud of you, Devin, and I am as well."

And after a brief but pregnant pause he then went on to add, "Unfortunately I doubt that the Board of Trustees, who have the final say, would see the matter in quite the same way."

And so that was that. Either I conformed to the rigid standards of the highly conservative Old Guard... or I would be summarily dismissed.

❧ ❧ ❧

I was heading on back to my own office, thinking over everything Henry had just had to say in my review, when I latched onto his comment about my fellow faculty members "for the most part" accepting me as I am. And I couldn't resist an ironic chuckle, for I knew damn well that a number of them had some serious reservations about me. It wasn't just my long hair, blue jeans and casual manner of presenting myself that sometimes upset them either. It was more my cavalier attitude towards academia. I simply didn't take my job quite as seriously as the rest of them did.

But more than anything else it was the fact that I was a legacy appointee that had turned some of my colleagues against me, and one in particular had made it perfectly clear that I had a long way to go if I ever hoped to earn his approval. His name was William Watson, and due to the dozens of articles and four books that he'd published, not to mention the impressive amount of grant money that his research projects brought in, he was most definitely the unrivaled "star" of the department. Or at least he had been until I showed up, that is. And therein lay the problem, because from the very beginning he was jealous, not only of my reputation as a globe-trotting adventurer, but also of all the regional media attention that my legacy appointment had generated. So whenever he had the opportunity he liked to find subtle, I might even go so far as to say "devious" ways to undermine my credibility. And because all academic departments are to a certain degree political, he had a number of ardent admirers among the faculty who supported him in that endeavor. So in spite of Henry's positive assessment of my relationship with my colleagues, as well as the fact that every last one of them was friendly to my face, I'd learned early on to keep an eye on my back.

❧ ❧ ❧

I was sitting in the shade of one of the many stately oaks that graced the main campus green, marveling at how strange it was not to have hundreds of college students milling about, when my good friend and colleague Lily Wilhelm came strolling briskly up.

"You're not going to believe this," she said with her usual sunny smile, brushing away a lock of prematurely gray hair that had blown across her cheek.

"Well at least give me a try," I told her. "Maybe I'll surprise you."

"Okay," she replied, easing down beside me. A petite and yet well-toned mid-forty year old in tan cotton shorts and a blue chambray shirt, she was the director of the Botany Department's rather modest conservatory, as feisty and high-spirited a woman as I'd ever known. "I think I may have just witnessed a miracle."

"Did you now? Then let's see. Was it somebody walking on water, or perhaps turning base metals into gold?"

"Nope," she said, shaking her head at my foolishness. "Nothing like that. And yet every bit as hard to wrap your mind around."

"Really?"

"Yes really. I've recently been hearing rumors about a woman who owns a botanical garden just south of here, down along the Seneca River, and her supposed ability to heal even the sickest of plants. So just out of curiosity, last week I took her a really spindly and listless philodendron I'd all but given up on."

She broke off and gave me a look that I couldn't quite interpret.

"And?" I wondered.

Reaching into the breast pocket of her chambray shirt, she drew out a Polaroid picture of a philodendron that was as deep green and healthy as could possibly be. "And this is the plant that I picked up today."

"You're kidding," I said, taking the picture from her and studying it carefully. "Nobody could produce results like this in a matter of days. Are you sure it's even the same plant?"

"Without any doubt whatsoever."

Well I'll be damned, I thought. This certainly bears looking into.

❧ ❧ ❧

The drive down along the Seneca River was absolutely stunning. It's not a long river by any means, only eighty-four miles from its headwaters to where it flows into the Little Scioto, but it runs through such beautiful countryside that it's been designated a Natural Scenic Waterway. And there was such a diverse selection of trees and shrubs and plants along its banks that I could easily see the allure the river valley must have had for Melissa Davis, the amateur botanist who owned and operated the botanical garden I was just then heading to. I'd spoken to her on the phone the afternoon before, because as I'd learned from my friend Lily Wilhelm she only opened her garden to the public from nine to eleven and one to three on Mondays, Wednesdays, and Fridays, and strictly by appointment, and she'd sounded absolutely delightful.

So needless to say my hopes were high as I followed the river south in my little red convertible, the mid-morning sun shining brightly down upon me from a deep and cloudless sky. I'd long been fascinated by the legendary figures in my field who were known to have had a nearly miraculous ability to nurture plants, so the prospect of meeting a woman who Lily believed had that same amazing talent was incredibly exciting for me. And I couldn't help but wonder if she brought about such dramatic results in the same way as two of my botanical heroes, Luther Burbank and George Washington Carver, both of whom were internationally renowned for being able to communicate with the natural world in mysterious ways that not only baffled their contemporaries, but also tread that fine line between the scientific and the mystical.

Not that I wasn't prepared for a letdown just in case. After all, history is full of supposed miracle workers who turned out to be nothing but clever charlatans, and I certainly wasn't about to embarrass myself by falling prey to one of those. In fact when I spoke to Melissa I hadn't even given her my name, because I wanted her to treat me exactly as she would treat anyone else—and not like an expert in the world of plants. That way she wouldn't be on her guard, and I'd be able to see her as the woman she truly was.

꽃 꽃 꽃

All precautions aside, I have to say that I was highly encouraged by my first impression when I reached my destination. There was a large brass sign set in stone along the road that read Eternal Bloom Botanical Garden, and as I turned into the driveway and passed through an open gate—helping myself to a map from the little rack attached to the grate—the scene I encountered was so unbelievably beautiful that my jaw damn near dropped open. The drive was lined on both sides by evenly spaced dogwoods in full spring flower, their pure white blossoms filling the air with a faintly hypnotic fragrance. Then a couple of hundred yards further on the drive entered an expansive roundabout, off to the right of which stood a nearly mythical Tudor cottage with a fieldstone foundation, heavy wood trim, and a steeply sloped gray slate roof. It was almost like entering the fictional setting of a J.R.R. Tolkien novel. And I was just about to turn my attention to the natural wonderland surrounding me when a fairly tall and slender dishwater blond in a short-sleeved work shirt and gardening smock came walking up a cobblestone path that must have led down to the river.

"Cute little car," she said as she came up alongside me.

"Thanks," I replied. "It's a lot of fun to drive."

"It's English, isn't it?"

"Right. An Austin-Healey Sprite. It doesn't have a whole lot of power, but it handles really well and uses very little gas."

"All the better," she said, her deep green eyes drifting

away from me to the maidenhair fern that sat on the floor in front of the passenger seat. "And I take it this is the plant that you're worried about?"

"Yep. I'm having trouble with brown edges and wilting leaves, and yet I can't figure out why. I mean I know a little about houseplants myself, and even through I've checked it for both pests and disease I can't find any sign of either one."

"Well let's have a look then."

So I bent over, picked up the plant, and reached it out to her. And while she was inspecting it I got out of my car and stood there beside her, taking note of the callouses on her hands, the dirt smudge on her cheek, and the sweat-stained blue bandana she had tied around her neck. I mean, this was definitely a hard working woman. And reserved too, somehow. Just don't ask me how I knew that, because I couldn't really say. In fact it was more of an intuitive appraisal than anything else. It's just that she had such high cheekbones and overall fine features that I couldn't help but think that she could have been really pretty if she'd wanted to be, but because of the way she presented herself she came across instead as more of a... shall I say "handsome" woman?

Be that as it may... "Give me a few days," she said, gently setting the plant on the hood of my car, "and I think I'll be able to help."

"Might I ask how?" I wondered.

And she gave me a rather mysterious smile. "Oh, it just needs a little tender loving care."

"Don't we all," I countered. "Could you maybe be just a little more specific?"

She held my gaze for a lingering moment, kind of like she was sizing me up or something, and then slowly shook her head. "Not until I've had the chance to actually work on the plant," she said evasively. "Besides, I'm not completely convinced that you've really made all that much of an effort to heal it yourself."

Needless to say that caught me by surprise. "And what makes you say that?" I asked.

And once again she gave me that mysterious smile. It was almost as if she was hinting at knowing something I didn't. "A number of things, to be honest," she said. "First of all it obviously hasn't been repotted for a while."

She broke off at that point, as if waiting to see how I'd respond to that. But since I had nothing to say to defend myself she then went on to add, "And anyway it's hard for me to believe that a man of your reputation would have so much trouble with a common houseplant."

Touché. "So you know who I am then?"

"Absolutely. Your arrival at Fairfield created quite a bit of publicity, you know, so it was fairly easy for me to recognize you from your picture in the paper. And given your level of expertise, I can't help but guess that you could've taken care of something as basic as a maidenhair fern if you'd really wanted to."

Now what in the hell was I supposed to say to that? I mean, not only was she right, but the fact that she'd seen straight through me was so unsettling that it left me at a loss for words. So I didn't even bother to try to come up with an explanation. I just gave her a somewhat sheepish but non-committal grin.

And that's when the fates stepped in to save me. A big yellow school bus came rumbling up the driveway, its windows full of the eager faces of what looked to me like younger teens.

"Middle school tour," Melissa said as the bus pulled up behind my car. "So I guess we'll have to leave things just as they are for now. I have your number, so I'll give you a call when your plant is ready, and you can come back and pick it up then."

"That sounds just fine to me."

She gave me a brief nod and started to turn away, but then something crossed her mind and she turned casually back around. "And since it's pretty clear to me that you've come here for some reason other than help with a sickly fern, please try to be just a little more honest from here on out. Can you do that for me, Devin?"

And properly chastised I told her that I would. It's just that she came across as being so enigmatic and intriguing on so many different levels that I was pretty damn sure that she wasn't being totally up front with me either. So we'd just have to see how that all played out.

❧ ❧ ❧

During my many years seeking out new plants I'd traveled to some of the most remote corners of the earth, by train, by plane, by boat and by car—not to mention by riding atop any number of exotic beasts of burden. But by far my favorite mode of transportation was simply going for a long and meditative hike.

And that's exactly what I was doing in the early afternoon following my first trip to Melissa's garden. I'd chosen a route that wound through campus and the eastern edge of town, and then up a steep rise and onto a little hilltop above Hopewell Lake, a local swimming hole that was a popular hangout for the college crowd. And what a lovely afternoon it was to be out strolling along too, low seventies, bright sunshine, and just enough of a breeze to keep me cool in spite of all the calories I was burning.

And as I moved easily ever onward, step by step and breath by breath, the air full of birdsong and rustling leaves, I thought over my first meeting with Melissa Davis. There was just something about her, some almost otherworldly or ethereal quality that made me feel as if it would be extremely difficult to get to know her on a personal level. But that alone wasn't the entire story. I also sensed that she was harboring some really deep secret, and that the reason she'd struck me as being so reserved was that she was afraid of revealing whatever that secret was to the world.

And why did I sense that? The answer is incredibly simple. Because as if by some magical force I'd always been drawn to botanists who worked outside the generally accepted parameters of the field, and not only acclaimed scientists such as Luther Burbank and George Washington Carver either, but also the highly secretive native shaman I'd been fortunate enough to get to know over the years. And it appeared to me as if Melissa Davis had that same unexplainable aura about her, that seemingly natural spiritual gift that elevated her above the norm. I can't really pinpoint exactly how I knew that, but there was certainly no escaping the fact that I did. In fact I knew it as surely as I knew the breath that was right then rushing in and out of my lungs, and in and out of my lungs, my heart beating out a steady rhythm that was perfectly in sync with my stride.

❦ ❦ ❦

What I liked most about my office was the oversized window with the wide oak sill and southern facing, for it acted almost like a little greenhouse for the numerous plants I'd lined up there. Bending over them with my brass watering can in hand, I gave each one a great deal of attention as I went, and I'm glad to be able to report that all of them were bright green and thriving.

Not that my office didn't have a few other attractive attributes as well. For one thing it was located on the perimeter of the main campus green, in one of Fair-field's oldest and most historical buildings, Rutherford Hall, a majestic brick structure with elaborate cornices and stone-inlaid corners. And on top of that it was a rather large and well-ventilated office too, with a really high ceiling and an abundance of antique cherry trim. So it shouldn't come as too much of a surprise that even though I could never really see myself being totally at ease cooped up in any office, as long as I had no other choice I was lucky that it was this one.

I was busying myself while waiting on the arrival of one of my favorite students, a sophomore by the name of Molly O'Grady who'd remained in town after the school had shut down. She was a first generation college kid with a great deal of potential but a major stumbling block. Because of her rather modest background, and the fact that she'd never received a whole lot of family support when it came to her education, she suffered from a certain degree of low self-esteem, and struggled to believe that she actually had what it took to succeed academically. So during the spring semester I'd more or less taken her under my wing, and had been counseling her pretty much on a weekly basis. In fact even though school was no longer officially in session she'd taken it upon herself to come up with a botanical project for the summer, monitoring the algae buildup along the west-ern shore of Hopewell Lake, due to the runoff of chemi-cal fertilizers from the area's abundance of farmland. And I'd readily volunteered to advise her on her work.

"So how's it coming?" I asked after she'd shown up and we were seated at my desk. She was a frizzy haired redhead in bellbottom jeans and a baggy white peasant shirt, the kind of outfit that was pretty common among the college kids of that highly free-spirited era.

"Slowly," she said. "It's far too early in the growing season for any algae to appear on the lake, so I'm basically just reviewing the research that's already been done."

"And from what little I've been able to find there isn't a whole lot of it, is there?"

"Not really," she said, her brow furrowing in disappointment. "So it must be a relatively new problem. Either that or nobody's ever really cared about it before."

"Well maybe that's a good thing," I told her. "Because if no one's ever really looked into it then you could be a forerunner in that particular field."

That appeared to come as a bit of a shock. "I could?" she said in a voice tinged with doubt.

"Absolutely. And that might very well provide you with the foundation for a career. If, that is, you plan to continue with this line of work."

"Really?" she said, obviously pleased, although perhaps somewhat skeptical, as if that possibility was simply too good to be true.

"Sure. In fact that's often how it's done. Take me, for example. The only reason I'm even here at Fairfield is that I did a lot of original work when it came to discovering new plants."

"And do you really think that I could do original work too?"

"Well, from what you were just now telling me, you already are."

She pursed her lips as she thought that over, and then broke into a great big smile. In fact she was so delighted to learn that she might already be taking the first tentative steps towards a career as a botanist that as she was leaving my office a little while later she gave me a spontaneous hug. And it made me feel so good to know that I was having such a positive impact on her that my life here at Fairfield suddenly seemed a hell of a lot more worthwhile. And for the moment I damn near forgot about all of the negative bullshit I had to put up with just to hold on to my job.

※ ※ ※

I was just leaving Rutherford Hall when Lily came hurrying up the brick walkway towards me, a somewhat anxious look on her face.

"Glad I caught you," she said as we met under the boughs of a massive oak tree. And then, after looking around as if to make sure that we were alone, she asked me if I'd seen this month's issue of The American Journal of Botany.

"Can't say as I have. I mean you know me. I'm not really an academic in the traditional sense of the word."

"Well you'd better give it a look," she said, "because it contains an article I think you need to read."

"Seriously?"

She gave me a solemn nod. "Your good buddy William Watson wrote it, and even though he doesn't mention you by name, I'm guessing you were the inspiration behind it."

Oh shit. Lily was my trusty confidant when it came to departmental matters, so if that article had her all wound up I could only begin to imagine the impact it would probably have on me. "And what, dare I ask, does he have to say?"

"Oh, it's just another one of his typical rants. He's bemoaning the direction our field is taking, mainly due to some current research on psycho-active plants that he refers to as to being unduly esoteric, and therefore unworthy of serious scientific consideration."

Yep. A comment like that was no doubt meant to be a slap in my face all right. So I told Lily that I'd most definitely look into the matter. And she merely gave me another nod and then quickly changed the subject.

"So have you been out to see Melissa Davis yet?"

"Just this morning," I told her. "I dropped off a maidenhair fern that needs a little work."

Her hazel eyes narrowed just a bit in response. "And so what do you think? Does she seem at all genuine to you?"

As a matter of fact she did, but I wasn't quite ready to commit to that yet. So all I said to Lily was, "It's much too early to say for sure. We'll just have to wait and see."

And God bless her. She had such a high degree of faith in me that she simply took me at my word.

✻ ✻ ✻

Early the next morning I pulled into an overlook along the Seneca River a mile or so upstream from Melissa's garden, where I parked my little red sportscar and unloaded my ten-foot kayak from the lightweight trailer I was hauling. I'd already dropped my hybrid bike off at Big Walnut State Park, not too far south of Eternal Bloom, locking it to the base of a picnic table near the boat ramp, and was now about to head out on a little recon mission. And why would I do that? Because my suspicions about Melissa were so very strong that I somehow knew that if I had any hope of uncovering her secrets I'd have to go about it covertly. I mean if I was right, then there was no way in hell that she'd ever take the risk of revealing those secrets herself. The results would simply be too overwhelming.

It was one of those days that was getting off to a rather gray and drizzly start, but I didn't care. I was wearing my swimsuit and a quick-drying nylon t-shirt, so it didn't really matter to me if I got wet or not. Plus

I'd brought along a wide-brimmed canvas safari hat that I then put on, not so much for the rain protection, but so that my face couldn't readily be seen. And after sliding my kayak down off the shore and into the water, I walked in knee deep, climbed into the cockpit, and let the moderately fast current sweep me away.

And what a wonderful little adventure it turned out to be too, letting the river supply all the power while I merely dipped my paddle into the water every now and again, either to keep my little kayak pointed directly downstream, or to maneuver it over to whatever point of interest happened to catch my attention. It was a far cry from my days of running some of the wildest and most remote rivers in the world, where I had to keep a constant eye out for rhinos, and hippos, and even the occasional crocodile. In fact I was enjoying myself so much that I was a little disappointed when I began to see, not more than a few hundred feet ahead, the natural growth along the shoreline giving way to the sculpted beauty of a botanical garden. So I steered my kayak over to the far side of the river as an extra precaution in case Melissa was out and about, and carefully looked for a place where at some point in the future I could pull it up onto dry land and conceal it.

And luckily the foliage was so very lush that I saw any number of attractive possibilities. So I chalked my mission up as an unqualified success as the current carried me swiftly on by, and then downriver towards Big Walnut State Park, where I'd drop off my kayak, get on my bike, and ride on back up to my car.

🌿 🌿 🌿

The little bungalow I was renting stood on a heavily wooded one acre lot right on the outskirts of town, but only about a third of a mile from campus. So not only did I have a great deal of privacy—which I absolutely cherished—but I was also close enough to work to either walk or ride my bike. And that's just the way I liked it. True, there was only a living room, a small kitchen, a bedroom, and a bathroom, and having moved in at the tail end of my vagabond days I didn't have a whole lot of furniture yet. But I kind of liked that too. Not that I'd chosen a monastic life, mind you. It's just that I'd always preferred to keep things simple.

I was sitting in my favorite chair, an antique oak rocker with a woven cane seat, having just finished reading the article in the American Journal of Botany that Lily had been telling me about. And she couldn't have possibly been more accurate in her appraisal. It was clearly a not-so-veiled attempt to undermine my credibility all right. In fact even though William Watson did indeed refrain from identifying me by name, he went so far as to make liberal use of overviews of my work to illustrate his claims.

And not only that, but there were a few additional aspects of his argument that sounded all too familiar as well, because they echoed some of the other recent critiques of the research being done into psycho-active plants. The only problem was that he passed them off as ideas of his own, which of course was a serious breach of the rather rigid rules of academic writing.

And that was an ethical lapse I most definitely felt I should look into a little more thoroughly.

❧ ❧ ❧

Later on that afternoon I made a quick trip over to Fairfield's rather modest conservatory to meet with Lily and see what more I could learn about the philodendron she'd taken in for Melissa Davis to heal. It was an L-shaped glass structure that offered specialized growing conditions for a permanent collection of botanical species that were used in teaching and research, everything from trees to cacti to succulents and ferns, and even a number of tropical plants. And after wandering through a couple of really warm and humid rooms I found Lily back in among a selection of wild flowers, testing the soil for nutrients.

"How's it looking?" I asked as I came up beside her.

And after setting down the soil meter she'd been reading, she smiled up at me and said, "It could use just a little more potassium, but otherwise it's just fine."

"As I assumed it would be," I told her, "knowing what pride you take in your work."

She passed off that compliment with a wave of her hand. "Just earning my keep," she said modestly. "The philodendron's back in the potting shed, so come with me and you can give it a look."

And with that she led me over to the far end of the building, where there was a separate little room full of clay pots, gardening tools, and at least a dozen bags of rich black soil. Not to mention the healthy green philodendron sitting in the middle of the wooden work bench.

"And what kind of shape did you say it was in when you gave it to Melissa?"

"Really bad shape," she said with an incredulous shake of her head, "although I know that must be hard to believe."

And if anything that was an understatement, for the plant was now in absolutely perfect condition, so the degree of healing that had to have taken place in such a short time was not only hard to believe, but it seemed to me to be an outright miracle.

❦ ❦ ❦

The moon was approaching half full that night, and the sky was essentially cloudless, so there was just enough ambient light that I didn't even have to wear my headlamp when I went for a stroll along the hike and bike trail that passed no more than a few hundred feet from my house. And since it was an old abandoned railroad grade, and therefore more or less straight and flat, it made for some really effortless walking. So once I'd established a fluid and rhythmic stride, step after step after easy-going step, I quit paying attention to my surroundings and allowed my mind to wander.

I was thinking about my life here at Fairfield College compared to the nomadic life I'd left behind. And to be perfectly honest I'd have to say that I found it to be somewhat lacking. I mean I loved the teaching part, the interacting with the fresh young minds and the ever hopeful attitudes of those just starting out. But an awful lot of the rest of it was just plain bullshit. The politics. The backbiting. And the extremely narrow approach a lot of my colleagues too often took to this world. In fact the sad reality was that it sometimes drove me to kind of a restless despair.

And that's exactly why I was so fired up to have come across Melissa Davis. It was far too early in the process of getting to know her to say for sure, but I had an incredibly strong intuitive feeling that discovering the mystery at the heart of her healing skills would reaffirm my faith in the botanical legends whose non-traditional work had inspired me to enter this field in the first place. And not only that, but immersing myself in the challenge of unraveling that mystery would make my time here at Fairfield much more of a rejuvenating adventure than it otherwise would have been.

And so as I walked along breathing in the cool night air, a sky full of billions of stars shining brightly above me, I couldn't help but feel a renewed sense of, not only hope, but purpose as well. And with that in mind I picked up my pace and head straight on back home.

2

A couple of days later I arrived at Eternal Bloom just after one o'clock in the afternoon. Melissa had called the day before to tell me that my maidenhair fern was now healthy and ready to be picked up, so I was pretty damn anxious to see the results. And since she was nowhere to be found when I first pulled in, I parked in front of her charming little Tudor cottage and treated myself to a quick walk around the front part of her garden.

And even though I know this may sound just a little overdramatic, I soon began to feel as if I'd somehow been transported to a completely different world. In fact the natural offerings surrounding me were so numerous and varied that I'll spare you the long list of specific names and merely give you the general classifications. Along with a wide selection of decorative trees, there were stands of hardwoods and evergreens, shrubs and bushes of every size and shape, and patches of both annuals and perennials galore. And that doesn't even begin to take into account the rock gardens, the ponds, the waterfalls, and the many metal and ceramic sculptures artfully displayed throughout. In short, it was a botanical wonderland of stunning proportions, every last bit of it in immaculate condition. So I couldn't have been any more impressed as I headed on back up to my car.

And that's when Melissa suddenly came into view, appearing almost ghostlike from between two enormous blue spruce in a cream-colored t-shirt and white overalls, her dullish blond hair pulled back and tied into a short ponytail. "So what do you think?" she asked with a sweep of her arm to indicate the entirety of her garden.

And as I was telling her how very beautiful I thought it was I couldn't help but notice how listless she looked, kind of run down, or worn out, as if she hadn't been getting nearly enough sleep or something. Which oddly enough played right into my suspicions about her plant-healing skills, and reinforced my belief in the need to learn about them covertly. Mainly because I now doubted more than ever that she'd be willing to tell me about them herself.

And the rest of our conversation that day left me even more convinced of that than ever. She'd set my fern on a rustic little bench a few feet away from my car, and the condition that it was in was nothing short of amazing. I mean its leaves were so very green and shiny that it was hard to imagine that it had ever been sick in the first place.

"So what did you have to do to it?" I asked as I held the plant up to inspect it more closely.

And she merely shrugged. "Not a whole lot, really. It was just a little root-bound and needed a few more nutrients, so I replanted it into a bigger pot in my special soil and mineral mix. And luckily that seemed to do the trick."

Yeah right, I thought, knowing full well that there had to have been a hell of a lot more to it than that. So I doubled down by getting a little more aggressive. "And that's it?" I said. "You didn't have to do anything else?"

And once again she merely shrugged, although I could tell by a fleeting look in her eye that she was suspicious about my reason for pushing the matter. And since I didn't want to take the risk of alienating her I decided to back off all together. "So what do I owe you?" I wondered.

And much to my surprise she seemed to find that amusing. "Nothing at all," she said as if that should have been obvious. "I do it purely out of my love for nature. In fact I might even go so far as to say that caring for plants is my life's calling."

"Well thank you," I told her. "That's very kind of you. And yet I have to admit that I find it rather odd, since from what I understand you don't charge people for coming in to tour your garden either."

"Nope. I'm happy enough just to share it with others. And you can't really put a price on that."

And even though I greatly admired that attitude, I still somehow felt compelled to ask, "So how do you pay for everything? I mean, I know damn well that it takes a lot of money to maintain a garden this size. Are you able to get grants, or donations or something?"

She slowly and gently shook her head, and then eased into a wry, even kind of evasive smile. And once again I took note of how tired she looked, especially around her eyes. "Let's just say that I'm financially stable, and that I'd simply prefer to leave it at that."

And that, of course, merely deepened the intrigue surrounding the woman, and heightened my desire to find out more about her.

⁂ ⁂ ⁂

My drive home that afternoon proved to be quite enlightening indeed, because Melissa's idealistic belief that healing plants was her calling was virtually identical to that of one of my historical idols, George Washington Carver. And not only that, but he too worked his magic purely out of a deep and abiding love for nature, and steadfastly refused to take any money for his services. And since many of the accounts of his seemingly miraculous ability to bring sickly plants back to life were extremely well documented—not to mention a legendary part of botanical lore—I felt more confident than ever about being on the right path to uncovering Melissa's secret methods... and more determined than ever to do exactly that.

⁂ ⁂ ⁂

I walked over to my office a little after eight the next morning, only to find a note in my mailbox that really pissed me off. It was a reminder from Henry Chandler about the final departmental meeting of the now-suspended semester, along with a brief outline of the agenda, which included this item: "The increasingly lax standards of appearance among faculty members."

And once again I was absolutely convinced that someone—either William Watson or one of his toadies—had filed a complaint aimed squarely at me, given that I was the only one among my colleagues who had long hair and liked to wear sandals and jeans. Everyone else was highly conventional in that regard.

And the funny thing is, the style in which I presented myself was actually somewhat misleading. Take my long hair for example. I hadn't grown it out because I wanted to fit in with the ever more influential counterculture. I'd grown it out because I'd spent nearly a year deep in the rainforests of the Amazon, where there was absolutely nowhere for me to get it cut. And since over that time I'd come to like the look, I'd simply left it that way.

Nonetheless, it was just one more bureaucratic aggravation that I had to steel my nerves and deal with. And one more reason to wonder if it was really worth it for me to put up with this shit merely to hold on to my appointment.

꙰ ꙰ ꙰

Lily and I were sitting on the flagstone patio of a quaint little bistro near campus, enjoying a mid-morning coffee break, when she gave me a rather soulful look and said, "It's really sad about those shootings down at Jackson State."

And since I rarely ever watched the news or read the paper all I could tell her was, "Sorry, but I don't have even the slightest idea what you're talking about."

She took a sip of coffee, peering at me over the top edge of her mug as if she couldn't believe that I was really that out of touch.

"You are most definitely a piece of work, Devin Douglass," she then said. "Don't you ever pay attention to what's going on in this world?"

"Sometimes," I told her. "But not very often. I usually find it too distracting in an unpleasant sort of way."

She shook her head as if she didn't know quite what to make of that. "It's a historically black college down south," she then went on to explain, "and yesterday two students were killed and twelve were injured while peacefully protesting the war. That makes six dead in a matter of weeks. And unpleasant or not, that's the kind of social injustice you can't just simply ignore."

"Well try to keep in mind," I told her, "that I spent the better part of eight years mostly isolated in areas so remote that I couldn't have paid attention to world affairs even if I had wanted to. And I guess I just kind of learned to like it that way. It helps to keep my life just that much more uncomplicated."

She released a long and exasperated sigh. "But what about the more positive aspects of what was going on during that whole time then? You missed out on all of that too, you know."

"Such as what?"

She paused to think that over for a moment before saying, "Such as The Beatles, for one. Don't you regret not being able to listen to their music back then?"

And there's no escaping the fact that she had me there. I'd never even heard of them until I was twenty-six and in Peru, having just come down from six months in the sub-alpine region of the Andes, when an old college friend sent me a news clipping about their appearance on the Ed Sullivan Show. And after that it was still another four or five weeks until I actually heard any of their music—although as soon as I did I became a nearly obsessive fan. So I went over that entire scenario for Lily, and then graciously conceded her point.

Not that doing so did anything to change my mind about keeping the greater world at a distance, though. Time and experience had made me kind of a loner, a misfit you might even say. And all in all that was just fine with me.

❧ ❧ ❧

Having hidden my kayak among a thick cluster of rhododendron, I took a few minutes to go over the map of Melissa's garden that I'd picked up on my first visit. Then I carefully made my way up from the river, coming to a stop just at the edge of a clearing in which stood an eerily beautiful solarium in the shape of a geodesic dome. It wasn't really all that big, maybe ten feet high and forty feet around, but it glistened so brightly in the midday light that it might have been a scaled down version of the almighty sun itself. And given my suspicions about Melissa's plant-healing methods, that simply couldn't have been more fitting. It was just a little before eleven, the time at which Melissa closed Eternal Bloom for two hours on the days that she allowed the public in, and if I'd read her correctly she'd be making an appearance just about any minute now.

So when she didn't show up until nearly eleven-thirty I was to say the least getting just a little impatient, not to mention a little stiff from hunkering down between two sizable juniper bushes. She had on an embroidered white pullover and blue jean shorts, and as soon as she opened the glass door to the solarium—releasing what sounded to me like the soothing music of Native American flutes—I raised the high-powered binoculars that hung around my neck.

And what I learned from gazing into that light-filled dome over the next hour or so was nothing short of amazing. There was a sunlit meditation mat in the very center of the circular floor, around which Melissa had placed a number of plants that appeared to be in various stages of health. At first she merely strolled slowly among them, as easily and naturally as a soft summer breeze, stopping to caress a leaf every now and again, and even bending over to gently rub a few against her cheek, her lips all the while moving as if she were talking to them, establishing a bond, connecting to each one in a very personal way. But eventually she drifted over to the meditation mat, where she settled down into the lotus position, closed her eyes, and folded her hands in her lap.

And that's when the strangest thing I ever could have imagined then happened. After a couple of minutes of quiet repose, Melissa slowly tipped her head back and raised her arms to the sky... and from out of nowhere the entire solarium suddenly started to glow.

And it was then that I knew beyond any doubt that I'd been right all along. Melissa Davis was a highly spiritual child of nature who believed in the universal power of the sun, and she was drawing upon its energy at the height of the day and passing it on to the plants in her care. That's how she nurtured them. That's how they healed. It was a synergistic combination of loving affection and the most powerful force in the entire cosmos: light.

And yet sadly enough there was a price to pay, for that whole process took so much out of her that by the time she'd given all that she had to give, and opened her eyes, and struggled to her feet... she was visibly and thoroughly drained.

❧ ❧ ❧

Having seen everything I needed to see, I waited until Melissa let herself out of the solarium and walked off in the direction of her cottage, and then just as I was getting ready to make a stealthy exit I heard a car pulling up in the distance. And even though that ordinarily wouldn't have been any big deal, a look of such deep concern came over Melissa's face that I decided to risk being discovered by following her to find out why she seemed so very troubled.

And boy am I ever glad that I did, for what took place over the rest of that early afternoon was the catalyst for setting my entire life off on a path that was a world removed from the one that I was just then walking. Staying well behind her, I moved from cover to cover until her cottage and driveway both came into view, at which point I squatted down behind a row of boxwood shrubs and watched as Melissa engaged in conversation with a man in a dark blue suit who'd emerged from a Chevy sedan that had South Carolina plates.

And take me at my word, she didn't look at all happy about whatever they were discussing either. In fact she looked downright distraught. So when the conversation eventually came to an end and the man in the suit got back in his car and left, I decided that I had no choice but to reveal myself. I mean, how in the hell else would I be able to console the poor woman?

"Afternoon," I said as I straightened up and walked her way.

And I have to give Melissa a whole lot of credit. In spite of the fact that talking to the man in the suit had clearly left her shaken, she handled my sudden appearance with a great deal of composure.

"Now where in the world did you come from?" she said by way of hello.

"Oh, I was just out running the river in my kayak and thought maybe I'd stop on by. Is that okay? Or is this a bad time?"

And it was that last question that ultimately did her in. At first she merely gave me a really blank stare. Then a single tear slowly made its way down her cheek. And finally her hands began to tremble a little.

So what else was I to do? Stepping forward, I wrapped an arm around her shoulder and said, "It's okay. Just go ahead and let it all out."

And for the next minute or so that's exactly what she did, leaning in against me and sobbing softly... until eventually drawing in a really deep breath and gently pulling away.

"I'm sorry," she then said, looking at me through tear-filled eyes. "I guess I'm just kind of at my wit's end."

I gave her a shallow nod to show that I understood. "And do you by any chance feel up to telling me why?"

She raised an arm to wipe her eyes on her sleeve, but didn't say anything in reply. And in the following silence I could tell by the tension in her body that she was engaged in a really intense internal debate—which ended as soon as I saw her relax.

"It's a pretty complicated story," she then said with a sigh, "and the only reason I'm willing to share it with you is that I can't help but think that you're one of the few people on this entire planet who'd be able to make sense of it all."

"Then have at it," I told her, "and let's see if you're right."

She gazed at me for a second or two, clearly hesitant to tell me in spite of what she'd just now said. And then she shrugged as if casting her fate to the wind and reluctantly began to open up to me. "That guy who just left here's one of the owners of an enormous southern nursery that supplies plants for many of the Big Box stores, and he's been hounding me relentlessly over the past few days. He somehow got word of my ability to heal plants, and at first he was really nice and seemed to show a lot of innocent curiosity about whether or not that was true. And yet once he became convinced that it was he started to become really aggressive."

"Let me take a wild guess. He wants you to come work at his nursery."

She gave me a quizzical if not slightly shocked look. "And just how did you know that?"

"Because growing plants commercially in an incredibly competitive and often cutthroat business, so there are those among the people involved who are willing to do just about anything to gain an advantage. And that of course includes hiring whoever can do the most to help them increase their profits."

"But I have no interest in abandoning my garden," she said calmly.

I gave her a sympathetic smile. "Well if you've already told him that, then what's the problem?"

"The problem," she began slowly, "is that he doesn't seem to be willing to take no for an answer. He first extended his offer earlier this week, and when I immediately turned it down he said that I should take a little time to think it over, and he'd come back to see if maybe I'd changed my mind."

"And that was today, I take it?"

The tears began to well up in her eyes again. "And when I really put my foot down this time, insisting that there was no way I'd ever leave here, he responded by threatening me.

"He what?"

"He threatened me."

"With physical harm?"

She looked down at the ground for a moment, and then back up at me, her eyes brimming over with fear. "Even worse," she said. "Jail time. According to what he was just now saying, while he was here the other day he came across a few of what he referred to as 'illegal exotics.' And when I was careless enough to tell him that I wouldn't know anything about that he gave me a really arrogant smirk, and then he got downright nasty. Lowering his voice to a menacing growl, he said that he'd give me until tomorrow to agree to his demands, and if I didn't he'd go to the USDA, who'd get a warrant to search my property and ultimately charge me with poaching. And that, of course, would effectively shut me down."

That sounded odd to me in a number of ways. "Well

first of all, I can't really see you poaching plants, but even if you have, then why not just get rid of them?"

"I can't," she said.

"Why not?" I wondered.

And at that point her entire body seemed to sag, whether out of fatigue or despair I couldn't really say. "Because I was being totally honest with him, Devin. I don't have even the slightest idea as to which plants they could be."

That momentarily gave me pause, simply due to the fact that it didn't seem possible. So what I eventually said to her was, "You've got to be kidding me, right?"

And she somewhat wistfully shook her head. "I'm not quite sure how to tell you this, because you're an actual botanist, an extremely well-educated man. But my relationship with my plants is almost exclusively personal. It exists on a highly esoteric, I might even say metaphysical level. I honestly know very little about them scientifically, in great part because I'm so sensitive to them that I've never really had to. I mean I'm sure you could identify each one by its Latin name. You know, its genus, or species, or whatever other terms there are. But I've never really had any interest in getting to know them that way. And even though over the years I've purchased hundreds of plants from various commercial sources, and collectors, and so on, I've always done so intuitively, by whether or not I felt a really strong attraction to them. And not because there was a specific type that I happened to be looking for. So if somebody ever sold me an illegally poached plant, there's no possible way that I'd ever know. It's simply not who I am."

Well in that case she was most definitely right. She did indeed have a problem. A really big problem. Luckily I believed I could probably solve it. "I'll tell you what then. When I was out roaming the world looking for new plants I had to be very careful about not mistakenly selecting those that were considered endangered, or invasive, or otherwise illegal to trade in or sell. So I have a pretty extensive background in that regard, and could very well be able to identify whatever poached plants you might actually have."

And I have to say that I fully expected her to feel pretty damn good about that. Unfortunately I was wrong. She didn't look even the least bit relieved. In fact she seemed to be every bit as distraught as ever. "So what's the matter now?" I asked.

"I'm still scared," she said bluntly.

"About what?" I wondered, getting a little impatient. I mean just how fragile could this woman be?

And yet as I was soon to find out, she actually did have some rather serious cause for concern. After another moment or two of hesitation, she looked me straight in the eye and asked if she really could trust me. "And I mean it, Devin, as much as I've ever meant anything in my entire life. My freedom truly is on the line here."

And even though I had no idea what I might be letting myself in for, I assured her that I was an extremely honorable man, and would never even consider betraying her—no matter what the cost.

And that clearly must have been the right response, for after yet another long and drawn out moment of contemplation she said, "All right then, follow me."

And with that she led me past her Tudor cottage and through an ivy-covered trellis to an area of her garden I'd never been to before, and eventually over to a quaint little cedar-shake structure.

"This is my potting shed," she explained as she opened the door to a pine-panelled room full of gardening tools, work clothes, and a rough-hewn maple work bench surrounded by stacks of terracotta pots and various bins of soil, all of it rather casually if not haphazardly organized. In fact it was kind of like walking into a mad scientist's lab or something. I mean she no doubt knew exactly where everything was, but to anyone else finding something in there would be one hell of a serious challenge. And yet as to what there was about the place that was making her so damn nervous... well, I didn't have a clue.

Until, that is, she bent over, grabbed the braided throw rug in the center of the floor, and tossed it aside to reveal a hidden trap door. "This is what I'm so concerned about," she then said.

And as she threw open that door the powerful glare of a cellar full of lights come instantly flooding out, the air suddenly so full of a rich sweet scent that I didn't even have to look all the way down in there to realize the full extent of her problem: Melissa had herself a rather impressive marijuana-growing operation going on here.

"So at least I now know where you get some of your funding," I said as she lowered the trap door and slid the braided throw rug back into place.

And as she straightened up she gave me a really sour look. "That's not it at all," she told me. "In fact I'd never even think about selling what I grow. It's all purely for medicinal purposes."

I can't actually say that I was skeptical about that, because she sure as hell didn't strike me as being your typical drug dealer—and yet I still felt as though I should ask if perhaps she could explain just a little bit further.

"I'd be happy to," she said. "But not in here. It's too nice a day to be inside."

And with that she led me out of her potting shed and down a path bordered by wildflowers to an ornate concrete bench that sat next to a pond laden with lily pads. "It all started two years ago when my aunt was diagnosed with Parkinson's," she began as we both took a seat. "She's long been widowed and has no kids, so I've taken on the responsibility of looking after her. And the more research I did into her Parkinson's, the more I realized how therapeutic treating her with marijuana could be. It would help to ease her pain, relax her stiff muscles, and even lessen the tremors she suffers from."

"So why not just buy it out on the street?" I wondered. "I mean it may be illegal, but it's still pretty easy to come by."

"You know," she told me, "I did consider doing that. But for one thing it's expensive, and for another I had no idea how to go about finding a reliable source. Besides—"

And breaking off she looked at me as if she was a little uneasy about saying anything more. "Are you absolutely certain that I can trust you?" she then said.

"Well if you can't it's too late now," I told her.

And she gave me a knowing smile. "Good point," she admitted. "All right then, here goes. Most of the information I dug up about Parkinson's came from an old friend of mine who just happens to be a doctor. And not only that, but she's a social progressive, maybe even kind of a renegade, who runs a free clinic down in Columbus. And when I told her that I was thinking about buying some marijuana for my aunt she got all excited, because as she was quick to tell me it also helps in treating people with endometriosis, fibromyalgia, Crohn's disease, and many other chronic conditions as well. So we right then and there made a pact. If I'd grow it and use it to help my aunt, she'd split the cost with me and use it to help some of her patients. And ever since then we've been doing just that."

"So if the USDA got a warrant to search your property..." I said, letting my voice trail off.

"Exactly," she told me with an emphatic nod. "I'd not only be in some really serious legal trouble, but I'd lose just about every last bit of what I've worked so very hard for. And this garden means everything to me, Devin. It's both my heart and my soul. I honestly don't know what I'd do without it."

I reached over and gave her a quick pat on the knee. "Then what about this? Why don't I do a quick inventory to see how many illegal exotics I can find, and then we'll just take it from there. Okay?"

And she did her best to muster what turned out to be a rather forlorn smile. "I suppose it's about the only hope that I have," she then said in a voice that sounded anything but hopeful.

*   *   *

"Well," I told Melissa as we stood at the base of a stately white pine, "I did indeed run across a number of troublesome plants. You've got a saguaro cactus, a staghorn fern, and a few rare succulents you're not supposed to have. Plus there are a couple of others I'm not quite sure about. The only thing is, they're all so beautiful, and so perfectly placed in your garden, that it would be a terrible shame to have to remove them."

"But I don't have any other choice," she said, obviously saddened by and yet resigned to that fact.

And therefore I was really happy to be able to say, "Oh yes you do. I've been giving this some serious thought, and there actually is another way to go about it. I mean, it may be illegal for you to own those plants, but if they're being used for research purposes it's not illegal for Fairfield's Botany Department to own them. So all you really have to do is tell that damn nursery owner that those plants are on loan to you from the college as part of a project to determine how well they can be persuaded to grow outside of their natural habitat. And if he really presses you about that, simply have him give me a call and I'll verify that you're telling the truth. Are you willing to take that risk?"

And she didn't even hesitate before saying yes. "I've designed my garden based on the organic principles of harmony and balance," she then told me, "and not only do I take a great deal of pride in that, but I'd be willing to do just about anything to maintain the natural order I've established."

"So does that mean that we'll go with the plan I just suggested?"

And for the first time since I'd revealed myself I saw a gentle light rise up in her eyes. "As of this very moment it's you and me against the world," she said.

And to seal the deal we even shook hands on that.

3

The final departmental meeting of the semester was held in the usual stuffy conference room off of Henry Chandler's office, and given the fact that we were about to address "the increasingly lax standard of appearance among faculty members" I had to fight back a chuckle as I looked around the table. For what I saw were seven heads of close-cropped hair, one three-piece tweed suit, four sport coats—two with elbow patches—and a couple of button-down shirts with ties. And then of course there was long-haired me in jeans and a loose-fitting cotton pullover that had been woven by a native artisan in the mountains of Columbia. So needless to say, the primary object of the meeting was obvious to the point of being absurd.

And not only that, but the somewhat awkward, shall I say faux-friendly atmosphere made me think back to the last official gathering I'd attended before abandoning my travels and moving to Fairfield. It had taken place around a roaring fire in the jungles of Peru, and involved me and a half dozen genuinely friendly tribal elders who'd come together to discuss the ever-increasing threat of deforestation to their beloved homeland.

And the stark contrast between what I considered to be the petty and the profound was suddenly so readily apparent that I once again wondered why in the hell I'd decided to subject myself to all of this bullshit in the first place. In fact it was all I could do not to simply get to my feet and walk out the door. And if the main reason for my even taking this position hadn't been to honor my grandfather and his legacy, I have no doubt whatsoever that I would've done just that.

*** *** ***

In spite of the fact that the spring's final faculty meeting had truly tried my patience, it had actually ended on a really positive note, in that Henry Chandler had asked me if I'd please stick around for a moment afterwards. And even though I was a little reluctant, since I'd assumed that he merely wanted to reinforce the rather stern lecture on academic propriety that he'd just delivered, I was pleasantly surprised when that turned out not to be the case. For he actually wanted to tell me something that I was more than happy to hear. Unbeknownst to my student Molly O'Grady, I'd applied to the department for a small stipend to help her with her research into the algae problem at Hopewell Lake, and he just wanted to let me know that it had been approved. It wasn't a whole lot, just two hundred dollars. But to a poor college kid in 1970 that was a pretty good chunk of money. And on top of that the timing couldn't have possibly been any better, because she was already scheduled to stop by for our weekly meeting later on that afternoon.

So I was pretty excited to see her when she showed up just as planned. Breezing into my office in striped bell bottoms and a light gray tunic, her frizzy red hair highlighted by a daisy she'd stuck behind her left ear, she took a seat opposite me at my desk and immediately broke into a smile.

"Good news," she said, setting the beaded macramé shoulder bag she often carried on the floor right next to her chair. "A faint sheen of algae has begun to appear along the shoreline, so I can really get down to some serious work now."

"That is good news," I told her. "And I have some good news too."

She gave me a quizzical look, obviously clueless as to what that might be.

So I simply went ahead and told her. "Well you see, I thought maybe you could use a little financial support this summer, so I applied for a stipend to help you with your research. And"—I slid the check across my desk—"I just found out that it's been approved."

And as she looked down at the amount of that check her jaw fell open and a light mist began to rise in her eyes. She wasn't quite able to think of anything to say, though.

So I took the opportunity to continue. "I also think that this is a cause for celebration," I told her, "so I'd like to take you and your boyfriend out to dinner sometime. Would that be all right with you?"

And that briefly left her speechless too, although when she did eventually find her voice she gave me a thankful nod and said, "That would be wonderful. When did you have in mind?"

"Oh, I suppose the sooner the better. How about tomorrow night?"

"It's a date," she said, briefly bending over to stick the check in her shoulder bag. Then she stood up and came around my desk. And for the second time in the past week or so she gave me a spontaneous hug.

❦ ❦ ❦

Not long after Molly O'Grady left, Melissa Davis called. "I just wanted to give you an update," she said in a light and melodic voice.

"Well it sounds like something good," I told her, "so please go right ahead."

"Okay then, that nursery owner showed up a little while ago, all arrogant and pushy and ready to put even more pressure on me to come to South Carolina and work for him. So I took your advice and really played up the fact that the poached plants he came across were part of a Fairfield research project."

She broke off and I could almost see her smiling. "So I take it that means that it worked then?"

"Like a charm," she said. "He didn't even bother to put up a fight. He just glared at me for a moment or two, and then turned around and left. And from the really pained look on his face I'm pretty sure that he won't be back."

"Congratulations," I told her. "That has to come as a huge relief."

"Indeed it does," she said. "And do you know what would make me feel even better?"

"I can't even begin to guess."

"Well I've been thinking. You're on summer vacation, right?"

"Yep. Free and clear. In fact I just came out of my last official meeting this morning."

"In that case, why don't you come out here and work for me part-time? I've gotten so busy that I could use some help with all the tours I have scheduled. And even more importantly, after what I've just been through with that damn nursery owner I'd like you to put together a detailed scientific inventory of everything in my garden. Would you have any interest in doing that?"

I didn't really, because it had been many a year since I'd had a lot of free time on my hands, and I was greatly looking forward to just kicking back and taking it easy. You know, maybe do a little research, on perhaps a little writing. But nothing too terribly taxing.

And yet the prospect of working right alongside Melissa did have a certain appeal, because it would give me the opportunity to learn more about her extremely mysterious relationship with her plants, so I decided that I should at least explore the idea. "Oh, I don't know. How many hours a week were you thinking?"

"That's completely up to you," she said, "as long as you work weekdays between nine to eleven and one to four."

"And what kind of a pay range did you have in mind?"

She thought that over for a moment before saying, "I'm really not all that concerned about the money, so I suppose something along the lines of what you're making at Fairfield, on a pro-rated scale of course."

And I have to admit that given those terms, I just might be interested after all. It's just that I wasn't quite ready to commit to that yet. "I'll tell you what then. Why don't you give me a day or two to think it over, and then I'll let you know. Can you do that for me, Melissa?"

"Take all the time you need," she said. "One way or another I'm not going anywhere. It certainly would be nice to have you around, though. I really could use the help."

"All right then. I'll give it some thought and let you know what I decide."

And for the moment we just left it at that.

⁂ ⁂ ⁂

In recognition of the fact that I was free of any departmental duties for the next few months, I called Lily the following morning and invited her out for a hike. And as an added incentive I told her that I'd be more than happy to let her choose the trial.

She most definitely picked a really good one too. It wound through a hilly and heavily wooded county park not too far north of Fairfield, and at that time of year, in full spring bloom, the scenery was flat out breathtaking.

"You know, history's full of famous people who sang the praises of a good long walk," I said as we shouldered our daypacks and headed out from the trailhead.

"Such as who?" she wondered, glancing over at me, her prematurely gray hair standing out in stark contrast to her lively hazel eyes.

"Aristotle for one," I told her. "He firmly believed that a casual stroll through nature helps to promote deep contemplation. Although my favorite is Thoreau, because he went even farther than that, saying that since humans are essentially a part of nature, a walk in the woods can lead to spiritual growth."

"I couldn't agree more," she said, picking up the pace a little. Petite or not, she was a real powerhouse, and so full of unbridled enthusiasm that it was if she simply couldn't bear to wait to see where the trail might take her.

And so we hiked along in silence for awhile, each of us off in our own little world, the only sound the burbling of a nearby creek and the rustling of the newly formed leaves in the breeze. Until...

"So how'd the faculty meeting go?"

"About like you'd expect," I told her. "I mean, this

whole idea of academic decorum was clearly initiated by William Watson in an attempt to discredit me."

"And do you think it worked?"

"In his eyes maybe, and in the eyes of his toadies. But to tell you the truth I don't think anybody else really cared all that much."

"Well what about you then? Did you hold up okay?"

"Sure. I've had to put up with all too many bureaucratic buttheads over the years, and I long ago decided not to let it get to me."

"And yet it would be nice if people weren't so damn self-serving to begin with, wouldn't it?"

She was absolutely right about that. Which got me thinking. Maybe I should just go ahead and accept Melissa's offer of a part-time job after all. I mean, it would not only be a really pleasant way to spend the summer, but it would help to keep my mind off all of the aggravating crap that went along with my life in academia.

And so just like that my decision was made.

✿ ✿ ✿

Melissa and I were strolling down a pine-needle path that led through a massive stand of Norway spruce towards a wide open field of daisies and clover. And no sooner had we stepped out of the shade and into the light than she slowed to a stop and turned her face towards the sky.

"Don't you just love sunlight?" she then said with a contented sigh. "It is, after all, the one and only source of life as we know it."

"Which is no doubt why our ancient ancestors worshiped the sun so passionately, "I told her. "They may not have understood it from a scientific point of view, but they sure as hell intuited its role in nourishing all living things."

"And therein lies the irony," she said. "Or at least one of them anyway. And Lord knows it's a big one."

"I'm afraid that I don't quite follow you."

She smiled over at me in a distracted sort of way. "And there's really no way that you could," she told me, "and that's entirely my fault. I spend so much time completely alone that my mind often tends to wander. I was just thinking about how the plants in my garden interact with the sun to not only remove harmful carbons from the air, but to also release life-giving oxygen in return."

And that led me to smile right along with her. "Then I think I may know where you're going with this," I told her, "even if that does mean jumping three or four thoughts ahead."

"Fossil fuels," she said, saving me the trouble, "which are actually nothing more than millions of year's worth of decomposed plants that have been highly compressed underground."

"And therefore the irony you were referring to," I told her, "in that over the incredibly short span of a little more than a hundred and fifty years we've dug up nearly all of those safely stored carbons and released them back up into the atmosphere."

"The absolute stupidity of it boggles the mind, doesn't it?"

"I'll say. And that's all the more reason for someone as insightful as you to establish a garden to enlighten the general public about the crucial role nature plays in sustaining our lives."

She gave me a rather forelorn look. "And that means an awful lot more to me than you realize," she said. "Let's just hope that it's not too little too late. Which reminds me. Thanks again for agreeing to come out to help me this summer. It really is becoming a bit too much for me to handle alone."

And with that she bent down to caress a bright yellow daisy petal, which must have been a highly emotional experience for her, because as she drew her hand away I saw her fingertips gently trembling.

※ ※ ※

Molly and I were sitting in a knotty pine booth at a local burger joint, which would normally be packed at this time of night, but was only about half full now that the campus had closed down.

"Here's to your stipend," I said to her, raising my pint glass of Guinness. And since she was only twenty, and too young to drink, she raised her glass of iced tea and we clinked.

"And thank you so much for applying for it," she told me. "I can really use the money."

"Not to mention that you also get a free meal out of the deal," I said as a joke.

And I was pleasantly surprised when she played right along with it. "Yes indeed. Oh lucky me. It's just too bad that my boyfriend came down with a cold. He would've really enjoyed scrounging a meal off of you too."

We both got a good chuckle out of that. "So," I said then, "let's talk about where you're going with your research."

And I was a bit taken aback at how serious she suddenly became. But then again, her uncommon dedication to her work was one of the reasons I considered her to be such a good student. "Well, now that the algae's beginning to build," she explained, "I want to go take samples to see what kind of chemicals are flowing in from the primary stream that feeds the lake."

"Good idea," I said. "And just when do you plan to start?"

She took a sip of iced tea. "I was thinking maybe sometime in the next couple of days."

"Then would you like me to give you a hand? I have all sorts of free time now that the semester's over."

"Sure," she said, her eyes lighting up. "I'm pretty busy tomorrow, so what about the day after that?"

"That works for me," I told her. "Not too early, though, because I'm technically on vacation and in no hurry to get going in the morning. So how about meeting me at the boat ramp at ten?"

"That would be great," she said. "And again, thank you so much. After struggling a little my first year or so here, I'm finally starting to feel as if I have some direction, or purpose I guess you might say. And that takes away a lot of the stress I've been under."

"Glad I could help," I told her. "I know how tough it can be to find your way at your age."

"Amen," she said with a shake of her head. And once again we raised our glasses and clinked.

❧ ❧ ❧

I began the next morning in a leisurely manner, having a quiet cup of coffee while re-reading some of my favorite passages in Silent Spring, Rachel Carson's groundbreaking study of how chemical pesticides wreak havoc upon the earth. And then as somewhat of a philosophical antidote to all of that depressing information, I went for a long and cleansing bike ride through the farm fields on the outskirts of town.

It was a beautiful time of day to be pedaling along too, the air still really crisp and clear, and the grasses along the side of the road shining brightly in a cover of dew. Not to mention that there was very little traffic to worry about, because the route I'd chosen was so far out in the open that I came across more Amish in horse-drawn buggies than I did people in cars.

And so I was more or less free to let my mind wander at will, my thoughts drifting from the interpersonal nonsense I was being forced to put up with at work to the enticing prospect of spending a good part of my summer in the botanical garden of the rather mysterious Melissa Davis. And as I eventually circled around and made my way back into town I realized that I was more than ready to take a break from the too often absurd pressures of academia, and get back to immersing myself in the natural world, which is the only place I'd ever really found any peace, and the only source of inspiration I'd ever truly had.

🌿 🌿 🌿

In preparation for my newly acquired part-time job, I drove out to Eternal Bloom in the early afternoon to be given my first really thorough tour. And just as I'd hoped it was a highly uplifting experience.

"These plants aren't just beautiful examples of what the natural would has to offer mankind," Melissa said as we wound our way down a pebbled path through a ground cover of marigolds, columbine, and other perennials too numerous to mention, most of which were nearing the peak of their full spring blossom. "They're what I like to think of as my companions, in that I not only communicate with them, but I learn from them as well. In fact the more receptive I am to what they have to teach me, the more willing they are to reveal their innermost secrets."

And having said that she went on to explain some of the more subtle aspects of their daily lives, such as which ones liked to live in close proximity to one another, what birds and/or insects each one attracted, and what nutrients they required to optimize their growth.

But it wasn't until she began to tell me about the Native American myth associated with the creation of Queen Anne's lace that I fully realized how she related to her plants on a level with which I was totally unfamiliar. So I asked her how in the world she'd ever come to know about that myth, thinking that if I could uncover a little more about her background I'd be able to better understand her highly unusual and yet compelling point of view.

And boy did that ever turn out to be the right approach to take. At first she merely gave me a little sideways glance, as if checking to see if I really did want to know, or if maybe I was just simply making idle conversation. And she must have somehow become convinced that I was totally sincere, because she then launched into a biographical overview that caught me completely by surprise. It was almost as if she'd been holding so much inside for so very long that once it all started to come out it took on a life of its own.

"It all began when I was just a kid," she told me, her eyes locking into a straight ahead stare. "For some reason I of course didn't understand at the time, I always preferred to wander aimlessly among the trees and plants on my family's estate rather than going to school. I simply felt more at ease there, more like my true self, as if that was actually where I was meant to be. And then at the age of twelve I planted my first garden, and tending it filled me with almost unspeakable joy."

At that point we came to an old oak park bench that faced a little waterfall bordered by ferns. So we sat down. She gave me a rather tired smile. And then she turned her eyes to the flowing water and continued with her story.

"Still, I did somehow manage to graduate high school, and even gave some serious thought to going to college. But I was so very restless at that formative age that I decided to take a year off to travel first. And as fate would have it that altered the course of my life."

She broke off then, thinking back, suddenly so lost in some distant memory that I felt the need to nudge her just a bit. "And why is that?" I wondered.

"Oh, you know how it is," she said with somewhat of a weary sigh. "When you first go out into the world on your own just about anything can happen. Or at least that's what it seemed like in my case anyway. And you have to remember, this was in the mid-50's, which was a fairly rebellious time. In fact in a mere matter of months I was exposed to so many elements of the emerging counterculture that it practically made my head spin. Kerouac and Ginsberg. Jazz and Be-bop. The beginnings of Rock n' Roll. I was so very enchanted by the world around me that I nearly lost my bearings."

And with that she turned to give me another little tired smile, holding my gaze for just a moment before going back to staring at the waterfall. "But then, and in retrospect it almost seems as if it absolutely had to happen, a guy I'd gotten to know at a poetry reading gave me a copy of the book Black Elk Speaks. And reading it suddenly changed everything, because it instantly validated the love for nature I'd felt deep inside ever since I was a child."

I'd heard of the book, but knew little about it, so I asked her if she'd please explain further.

"I'd be glad to," she said in a rather wistful voice. "After all, it opened up a brand new world to me. It chronicles the life of an elderly Sioux Holy Man and his visionary relationship with the natural world, and I was so spellbound by the spiritual insight he had to offer that I took it as a sign that some force beyond my comprehension was trying to tell me what direction my future should take. So I packed up and headed out to the Wind River Reservation in central Wyoming, where for the next couple of years I dedicated myself to learning about the miraculous powers of nature from a highly regarded Arapaho Medicine Woman, although that's an extremely superficial term that doesn't even begin to capture her elevated status among her people. And the ancient wisdom she had to offer not only spoke to my very soul, but also helped to clarify my purpose in life, ultimately leading to me coming here to Ohio, buying this property, and setting about planting my garden."

And falling silent again she looked up at the sun, and then told me that it was time for her to go, because she was scheduled to take a phone call soon. "But you go ahead and keep looking around," she said as she stood, grimacing a bit from the effort, "since the better you come to know my garden, the more helpful you will be."

And giving me one last little tired smile, she stepped off the pebbled path we'd been walking and slipped between the dark green boughs of two closely planted Colorado spruce, disappearing so suddenly that it was almost as if she'd never really even been there at all.

❧ ❧ ❧

A feeling of awe came over me as I continued with my now self-guided tour of Eternal Bloom. I mean it certainly didn't compare to the most magnificent botanical gardens I'd been fortunate enough to travel to over the years, such as the Kew Gardens in London, on the Jardin Botanica in Rio de Janeiro, but it was most definitely impressive nonetheless. There was just so much diversity in Melissa's collection, and such artistry in her overall design, that I was amazed that one woman could have conceived of it all. And not only that, but I was also really curious as to how she could afford it—especially since she first bought the property when she was only in her early twenties with no more than a high school education. Seriously. The money must have come from somewhere, and she did briefly mention her "family's estate." So my guess was that her parents had to be wealthy. And yet... I don't know. She certainly didn't come across as being a spoiled rich kid. Quite the opposite in fact. She struck me as being about as down-to-earth as anyone I'd ever known. So I decided to simply let the matter rest. Something told me that I'd eventually find out anyway. Only time would tell.

And if there was anybody who had a lot of that these days, it was most definitely me.

❧ ❧ ❧

Melissa came down off the front steps of her enchanting little Tudor cottage just as I was getting ready to leave. "So I'll see you tomorrow afternoon?" she said.

"Yep. I'll be here and ready to go at one."

"Well in that case let me give you a word of warning. I just got off the phone with a reporter from the Cleveland Plain Dealer who's been pestering me about doing a feature story on my garden. It's just that the last thing I need right now is any more publicity, because the attention I've been getting over the past few months has for some reason really gotten out of hand, to the point that I can hardly even keep up with all the demands already being put on me. The problem is, the more that I decline her offer, the more insistent she becomes. In fact she's every bit as aggressive as that damn nursery owner.

So I wouldn't be at all surprised if she just showed up and started asking questions. And as you well know, that could possibly lead to a whole lot of trouble."

"Not to worry," I told her, climbing into my little red sportscar. "If she does come out here I'll do everything I can to discourage her."

She gave me a barely discernable nod of thanks, and then simply folded her arms across her chest and stood there watching as I fired up my engine, shifted into first gear, and drove out of the roundabout and down the front drive, the bright white dogwood buds so very fragrant that I couldn't help but marvel at the many blessings that springtime has to offer us all.

❀ ❀ ❀

Lily and I took a late afternoon bike ride out into the countryside just north of town, stopping for a break along a section of the Seneca River that featured an impressive series of whitewater rapids.

"This is absolutely beautiful," I said, taking off my helmet and walking on down to the waterline, but not too close, because the current was dangerously strong.

"I'll say," Lily replied, running her hand through her mussed up hair as she strolled up right alongside me. You'd think that being prematurely gray would make her look older than her forty-some years, but it didn't. She was just so full of energy and enthusiasm, and so physically fit and active, that it merely gave her a rather distinguished look.

"I used to bring the girls here to picnic when they were kids," she told me, referring to her two daughters, who were now grown and gone, leaving her an empty nester. And since she'd long been divorced she was now very much on her own, and reveling in the freedom.

"Well I don't have a basketful of food," I said, grinning over at her, "but I do have a bag of trail mix that we can snack on."

"That would be great. I could use a bit of a boost."

So we sat down on the riverbank and shared my homemade blend of nuts and raisins and chocolate drops, all the while talking about whatever came to mind, our conversation wending here and there and everywhere until...

"So now that you've had the chance to get to know her a little," Lily wondered, "just what do you make of Melissa Davis?"

And I had to take a minute to think about that. "You know," I eventually said with a slight shake of my head, "I'm still not really sure. She has a gift. There's no doubt about that. But as to exactly what it is... well, I'm going to need a little more time to sort that out."

"Just be sure to keep me informed," she said, "because even though I've only met her twice, I find her to be fascinating. And I say that because I have a gut feeling that her ability to heal plants somehow transcends science and enters into the realm of the, I don't know, the mystical maybe?"

I couldn't have agreed more. There was just something about her, some unusual, dare I say magical quality that allowed her to be uncommonly sensitive to, and attuned to, the natural world that she loved so much. And even though I know this may sound incredibly selfish, I couldn't help but hope that the more time I spent working alongside her this summer, the more I'd be able to develop whatever innate abilities I might have along those lines. I mean, I had no grand illusions about becoming another Luther Burbank, or George Washington Carver, but I damn well knew that there was not only more to being a botanist than what I'd already learned from text books and lab work and even my extensive adventures in the field, but that Melissa Davis was intimately familiar with some other form of knowledge that went way beyond everything I'd been exposed to so far. And I was bound and determined to find out what that was, no matter how esoteric it might turn out to be.

Before bed that night I wandered out into my yard and lay down on the grass, staring up into the billions and billions of stars overhead, the air sweet with the scent of honeysuckle and the dark woods alive with the mating calls of insects and tree frogs and even an occasional distant owl. It was my way of bonding with the earth, immersing myself in its organic splendor and releasing all the stress and pressure of the day in the hope of a long and restful sleep.

4

When I drove out to the boat ramp at ten the next morning there was a light mist drifting across the surface of Hopewell Lake, the rapidly warming air still so very damp that I'd left the top up on my little red Austin-Healey. Molly wasn't there yet, so I merely sat on the beach enjoying the view until she came riding up on a battered old Schwinn.

"Morning," she said as she hopped off and put the kickstand down. She was wearing rubber flip-flops, high-cut jean shorts, and a black and gold Fairfield hoodie, her frizzy red hair looking a couple shades darker in the muted light of a cloudy day.

"All ready to go?" I asked.

"Absolutely," she said, so full of the enthusiasm of youth that I just had to smile. "I've even come up with a plan for collecting samples."

And having said that she gave me a rather sheepish look. "I mean," she then added, "if that's okay with you."

"That suits me just fine," I told her. "After all, this is your research project. I'm only here to help."

And that clearly came as a bit of a relief. "Then what I had in mind was for you to collect algae from just off the shoreline, and I'll wade out a little deeper and collect sediment from the Benthic Zone."

"The Benthic Zone?" I mused, suitably impressed.

And she was so very shy about having used the scientific term for the bottom lake that she then blushed a little, which I found to be absolutely charming. "Okay," she then said, her eyes bright with anticipation. "Let's get started."

And reaching into the kangaroo pocket on the front of her hoodie, she drew out a half a dozen little round petri dishes and handed me three. Then she bent over to set the other three on the sand and did something that caught me completely off guard. Grabbing the hem of her hoodie, she pulled it up over her head, revealing a skimpy little bikini top and heavily freckled shoulders.

"Off I go," she then said, draping her hoodie over the Schwinn's handle bars, picking up her petri dishes, and heading out into the lake.

And all I could do was marvel at her childlike innocence, wading out into the shallows half-naked as if it was the most natural thing she could possibly do, not a care in the world, her thoughts focused solely on the matter at hand.

Molly was sitting across from me at a wooden picnic table, labeling her petri dishes with a black felt pen, when she suddenly looked up and cocked her head. "Did you hear that?" she said.

"Hear what?" I wondered.

"That bird singing," she told me, obviously intrigued.

In all honesty I hadn't, until it sang out again, its lively little melody drifting across the water from the far side of the lake.

And in an instant Molly was on her feet, rushing over to her bike, unzipping the brown leather pouch attached to the back of the seat, and drawing out a small hand-held recorder. "Bird songs are a hobby of mine," she then said as she sat back down, setting the recorder on the table and turning it on. "And when I hear one I don't recognize I like to make a tape of it. That way I can find out what kind of bird it is later."

"Good idea," I said, and I was about to add something along the lines of what a unique and interesting young lady she was when a sudden flash of lightening crackled across the darkening sky, followed a nano-second later by a thoroughly intimidating rumble of thunder.

And that spurred the entire park into action. The beach had started to fill up by then, and everyone there immediately grabbed their towels and ran towards the open-sided shelter next to where we were sitting, among them two doctoral students I recognized from Rutherford Hall, but didn't know yet because my appointment didn't require me to teach graduate classes.

"Come on," I told Molly. "Let's get in the car."

So we hustled over and climbed into my Austin-Healey, breathing heavily from the effort, the air having grown so thick and humid that it wasn't long at all before the windows fogged up. Which was actually kind of cool, because it was as if we were safely cocooned in our own little world while riding out what ended up being a relatively short but seriously powerful storm.

And all things considered, it turned out to be quite the pleasant interlude too.

❧ ❧ ❧

"So the main thing I'd like to have you do," Melissa said, sitting on the front steps of her storybook Tudor cottage, "is to put together a scientific inventory of my entire garden."

"Does that mean that you'd like me to post little signs so that people can read the Latin names of whatever they're looking at?"

"Oh no, nothing like that," she cautioned. "To me that would merely intrude on the garden's natural beauty. I was thinking more along the lines of creating a detailed map to replace the more generic one that I offer the public now."

"Well that sounds easy enough," I told her. "I could use the existing map as a template and simply go from there."

"Whatever works for you," she said with a shrug, "although I'm sure I'll be interrupting you every now and again to help me with tours, and whatever else I may need you for."

"That shouldn't pose any problems," I told her. "It's not as if recording all those names is going to require a whole lot of concentration. I mean as long as I have a classification handbook to assist me with the names I don't know off the top of my head, it should be fairly easy work."

"That's exactly what I was hoping," she said with a smile. "After all, I don't want to put too much pressure on you this summer."

And it was all I could do not to scoff at that. "Believe me, after everything I went through before settling down here in Ohio, working for you should be a walk in the park."

"Literally," she said with a charming little laugh.

And it was then that I noticed a slight air of fatigue about her. But then again, it was early afternoon and she'd no doubt recently come from meditating among the plants that people had brought in for her to heal. So I really wasn't all that surprised. Although I do have to confess to being just a little concerned. She was simply too young to be looking so very run down, especially on a daily basis.

❧ ❧ ❧

I was wandering through the relatively small but efficient greenhouse at the center of Eternal Bloom, putting together a preliminary plan for classifying the wide variety of botanical species to be found there, when Melissa came walking in with a middle-aged brunette who was almost comically overdressed in a floral jumpsuit, open-toed sandals, and a burnished leather handbag. She looked like she could have been on her way to a fancy cocktail party, or an art gallery opening or something.

"Devin," Melissa said. "This is Mrs. Wellington. She'd like to have a look at my orchid collection, and since I'm incredibly busy at the moment I was hoping you'd be good enough to show her around."

And from the decidedly sour look on Mrs. Wellington's face, I could tell that she wasn't at all happy about being handed off to a common employee like me. Which became even more obvious when she then gave me a quick onceover before turning to Melissa to say, "And you're absolutely certain you won't be able to accompany me yourself?"

"Sorry," Melissa told her. "I really am pressed for time. Not to worry, though. Devin's a Botany professor who's simply helping me out this summer, so I'm sure he'll be able to answer whatever questions you may have."

Mrs. Wellington rolled her eyes at that, clearly put off about not getting her way, and I realized right then and there that she was so very spoiled that I was going to have to do whatever I could to restrain myself. I mean I've never had much patience with self-obsessed people, and yet for Melissa's sake I knew that I had no choice but to be nice to Mrs. Wellington anyway.

So when Melissa then politely excused herself and left I did my best to be as pleasant as possible. "And how is it that you're so interested in orchids?" I asked as I ushered Mrs. Wellington over to three evenly spaced rows of beautiful but highly delicate flowers in a breathtaking arrangement of sizes and shapes.

"Well you see," she said with a certain condescending air, "I've been competing in shows for a number of years now, so I'm always on the lookout for a new and exciting variety. And therefore, when I recently learned of Miss Davis, and her exceptionally well-reviewed garden, I simply thought that I'd stop by to see if she had anything that might capture my interest. And I must say that if these orchids are typical of the quality of her work, her reputation is very well-deserved indeed."

"And there are even more outside if you'd like to see them," I told her. "Is there any particular Genus or species you're attracted to?"

And I was more than a little taken aback when she seemed flustered by that question. "Genus?" she said as if the word was totally foreign to her. "Well, um, no. Or at least not one that readily comes to mind. I simply like orchids in general."

Now that's odd, I thought, given that most orchid

growers were almost fanatically devoted to at least one specific variety. And yet she was looking at me with such disdain that I decided not to press her on the issue.

"In that case, take your time to look around in here," I told her. "And when you're finished we'll go outside."

"That's very kind of you," she said in a dismissive tone, "but I'd much prefer to stroll the garden alone. That way I can take it all in at my leisure."

"As you wish," I told her with a slight but in my mind mocking bow, extremely grateful to be relieved of my duties. And yet instinctively suspicious of Mrs. Wellington too. There was just something about her that didn't quite ring true, and I was more than a little curious to find out exactly what that for now elusive something might possibly be.

❧ ❧ ❧

After leaving Mrs. Wellington alone in the greenhouse, I walked just far enough into the garden to be out of her sight. And then I circled back, secured myself behind the trunk of a loblolly pine, and prepared to wait for however long it might take until she appeared.

And believe me it happened a lot faster than I would've expected. In fact I wasn't even completely settled in when she made her way out into the open, where she took a minute to consult the map that she drew out of her handbag. Then she headed off down the pine-needled path that passed the outdoor rows of orchids, giving them no more than a cursory glance as she hurried on by in the direction of the solarium.

And as I discretly fell in behind her, the real fun truly began. Upon arriving at the clearing where the solarium stood, Mrs. Wellington looked around as if to make sure that no one else was there, and then walked up to the door and gave it a tug, exhibiting a great deal of frustration when she found that it was locked.

She certainly wasn't about to give up all together, though. Cupping her hands around her eyes, she then leaned in against one of the geodesic glass panes and peered intently into the interior, studying it carefully for what seemed like much longer than necessary to simply get a feel for the place.

And then, stepping back, she really began to get down to business. Scanning the perimeter of the clearing for a moment, she then walked in a straight line over to a dense stand of pin oaks and disappeared in among them. She didn't really go in all that far, though. In fact I could still kind of see her moving around, although she was obscured just enough that I couldn't really tell what she was doing. And yet whatever it was, she quickly finished and made her way back out into the clearing.

And at that point things really started to get a little strange. After taking no more than a step or two out of the trees, Mrs. Wellington abruptly stopped and took a swat at the air in front of her face. And then another. And another. And when she then began to frantically flail her arms at what I assumed was a single pesky insect of some kind, my thoughts drifted back to my days on the Alaskan tundra, where from the moment I got out of my tent in the morning until I crawled back in at night I was constantly being attacked by swarms of mosquitos and blackflies and gnats. "The deadly hum" I used to call it, and in addition to long-sleeved shirts and pants cinched at the ankle, my only hope was to wear a head net all day long. If not, my eyes and ears and nose, and at times even my mouth, would be instantly filled with bugs. Their presence was so very pervasive, in fact, that when I awoke at dawn every day there would be hundreds of them attached to the netting at the door of my tent. So needless to say I had little sympathy for

Mrs. Wellington's plight. If anything it merely added a little comic relief to what was otherwise a pretty damn serious situation. And the more that she flailed, the more I felt that she probably deserved to be bitten. In fact it seemed like a fitting punishment for all of her snooping around.

❧ ❧ ❧

After laying low until Mrs. Wellington eventually quit flailing at the air and then immediately scurried off, I walked over to the stand of pin oaks she'd disappeared into a few minutes earlier. And there I found, not more than ten feet in, and secured to the trunk of one of the trees, a small wildlife camera, the kind normally used for spotting deer, and game birds, and other objects of the hunt. It was pointed directly at the door of the solarium.

And that gave me an idea so very devious that I found myself breaking into a smile.

❧ ❧ ❧

I'd only been back in the greenhouse for a minute or two before the door swung open and Melissa walked in, looking more than a little embarrassed. "I am so sorry about sticking you with Mrs. Wellington," she said. "I honestly didn't know what else to do."

"That's okay," I told her. "It was no big deal. I have a whole lot of experience putting up with self-centered people." And yet I held off on saying anything about the wildlife camera. I mean why should I worry her? After all, I was pretty damn sure that I could take care of the situation myself. In fact given Mrs. Wellington's highly deceptive behavior, I was kind of looking forward to it.

"It's just that she was so incredibly overbearing that she was driving me crazy."

"Overbearing about the orchids, you mean?"

"Oh no," Melissa said, her eyes going wide. "That was just her starting point, and then she began to pester me with questions about my plant-healing methods. And she was downright pushy about it too. Seriously. The more I tried to steer the conversation back to the orchids, the more insistent she became. Until finally I simply couldn't take it anymore. And that's when I decided to turn her over to you."

"Well again," I said with a shrug. "It was no big deal. And to tell you the truth, I have a pretty strong feeling that we haven't seen the last of her yet, so if she does call to make another appointment just let me know and I'll take over from there."

And I have to say that the prospect of engaging Mrs. Wellington again was actually rather attractive in an idealized sort of way. I mean I wasn't at all sure as to what she was up to, but I knew damn well that it wasn't anything good. So being there to catch her in the act, so to speak, seemed like exactly what any would-be hero would look forward to doing. It must have been the latent romantic in me.

❦ ❦ ❦

Not long after I returned to my little bungalow Lily stopped by, and I could tell by the rather pinched look on her face that she was really upset about something. So I sat her down, made her a cup of tea, and asked her what was wrong.

"Just more bullshit from William Watson," she told me, shaking her head at the mere mention of his name. "I was watering plants in the conservatory earlier today when he came in to check on some goldenrod he's growing for a research project. And while he was there he rather snidely asked me if I'd read his newly published article in The American Journal of Botany."

"And did you tell him the truth?"

"I did indeed," she said, "although I was very diplomatic about it, mainly because I didn't want to piss him off. The last thing I need's for him to turn on me like he's turned on you. My job doesn't come with tenure, you know, so I'm in somewhat of a precarious position. In fact he was quick to remind me of that."

"He what?" I blurted, feeling the heat rise in my cheeks.

"Well to be perfectly honest I'd have to say that he was trying to intimidate me," she then admitted. "Not directly. He's far too sly for that. But the point he was making was clear as could be. After referencing his article he let me know that he was well aware of how close you and I have become, and he suggested that due to your highly controversial field of research I'd be better off distancing myself a little. After all, he reminded me, I have a performance review coming up in the fall, and he wouldn't want to see it turn out poorly."

"That bastard," I said. "I mean, if he wants to come after me, so be it. I can handle that just fine. But to drag you into all of this too? That's just flat out unacceptable."

"So what do you suggest that I do?"

"Well other than being careful not to antagonize the guy, I don't think you should do anything at all. Just go on ahead about your daily affairs. And please don't worry. I can take care of William Watson. Believe me I can."

"I sure hope so," she said with a little frown. "I love my job, and I'd really hate to lose it."

"Trust me," I told her, reaching over to give her a reassuring pat on the shoulder. "I simply won't allow that to happen."

And even though she responded with an encouraging smile, there was still just a hint of doubt in her eyes.

❧ ❧ ❧

Setting aside the most recent issue of The American Journal of Botany, I got up out of my antique oak rocker and headed off to the kitchen to get myself a beer, now more convinced than ever that William Watson had only a superficial understanding of the current research being done into psycho-active plants. And not only that, but to his additional discredit he'd clearly failed to acknowledge the statements of others when formulating his own opinions. In other words his article was a glaring example of shoddy scholarship at best, designed to do little more than jeopardize my standing in the academic department my very own grandfather had founded. And because of his exalted reputation in the field—not to mention the vast among of money his research projects brought in—he was just arrogant enough to think that he could get away with it too.

Unfortunately for him, I wasn't about to just passively stand back and wave the white flag. In fact I was bound and determined to do whatever I had to do, not only to defend myself, but to take the fight right back at him. And I had a pretty good idea as to just how to go about doing that too.

❧ ❧ ❧

A light rain tapped at my window as I lay I bed that night, trying to work through my frustration with William Watson's mean-spirited attempt to discredit my research into psycho-active plants. And what upset me the most was that his only cultural frame of reference was the recreational use of those plants among hippies, and bikers, and others who lived on what he considered to be the outer fringes of America's society. I mean he clearly had no knowledge whatsoever of how they could be used for the much more enlightening purpose of self-discovery and spiritual growth.

And that's exactly what had drawn me to them from the start. I was first introduced to their mystical powers deep in the jungles of Guatemala by a native shaman whose name, tribe, and specific location I prefer to keep to myself, so as to not risk exposing he and his people to any further Western influence. For by the time they reluctantly accepted me into their midst they'd already become aware that they were in danger of losing their age old cultural identity, and that was an ever more daunting prospect that frightened them to their very core.

And no one was more keenly conscious of the threat they were under than their highly revered shaman himself, a man whose position among his people went even beyond that of an iman, or a rabbi, or a priest. And how could that be in a culture that many here in the West would consider to be nothing more than the scattered remnants of an illiterate pre-historic society? The answer is about as basic as the dawning of the day: Because he served as an intermediate between the physical and spiritual worlds, a visionary who embodied both mystery and magic. Or in other words a prophet who could help to connect his people to whatever world lies beyond our own.

And because William Watson would have no doubt scoffed at that idea, and done everything in his power to subject it to ridicule, I realized that he'd never, ever be able to grasp the true significance of the shaman among his people, or the great depth of meaning behind his rituals and deeds. So I knew that it would have been foolish of me to even consider trying to win him over to my point of view.

But allow him to demean my research, or denigrate me in front of my peers? I simply wasn't about to let that happen. And so as the rain continued to tap at my window I rolled over onto my side and released a really deep sigh, knowing full well that an academic standoff with William Watson was in and of itself a petty and ultimately meaningless pursuit. And yet also all too painfully well aware that I really had no other choice.

5

❧

Mrs. Wellington returned to Eternal Bloom on a sunny afternoon a couple of days later, once again wearing a fashionable although somewhat garish jumpsuit, a paisley print this time. It was so very colorful in a cartoonish kind of way that she looked like she could have just stepped out of a Pete Max painting or something. And just as before she was every bit as haughty and standoffish too.

"How lovely of you to offer," she told me when I volunteered to help her complete the tour she said she hadn't quite finished. "But as you may remember I'd much rather look around on my own. That way I can seek out those aspects of the garden that are of the highest interest to me. Surely you must understand."

She was most definitely right about that. In fact I understood a hell of a lot more than she realized. So I

was more than happy to have her wander off all by herself, and even happier to shoulder the little daypack that
sat there beside me and follow along at a distance. And
as I fully expected she spent just enough time putzing
around to create a bit of a cover before heading off in
the direction of the solarium, and the stand of pin oaks
where she'd hidden her wildlife camera.

Little did she know that it was no longer there. In
fact it was in my little daypack. And as she was about to
enter those pin oaks I took it out, edging closer and
closer, and began to film her every move, feeling quite a
bit like a predator about to pounce on its prey.

Although the ultimate outcome was a lot less ghastly
than it was oddly comical. Upon seeing the camera
bracket, but not the camera itself, Mrs. Wellington was
visibly stunned, her cheeks turning a deep scarlet and
more than a hint of panic rising up in her eyes. And
that's when I stepped up from behind her, filming away,
and asked what I thought was the most basic of questions.

"So Mrs. Wellington, who are you really?"

And that came as such a sudden shock that at first
she merely burbled. I'm serious. She burbled. It sounded just like a babbling brook. And then she hemmed.
And then she hawed. And finally her entire body sagged
and she gave me a rather pathetic look.

"I'll tell you," she said in a voice acknowledging
defeat. "But only if you put that damn camera down."

❄ ❄ ❄

"A reporter!?" Melissa said, obviously aghast. "Please
tell me you're only joking."

And even though "Mrs. Wellington's" reaction to
being caught red-handed actually had been kind of

funny, I told her that no, I was just about as serious as I could be. "And not just any old reporter either," I then went on. "She's the one who called the other day about doing a feature story on you and your garden."

"Oh no," Melissa said, her face clouding over. "I really don't want to have to deal with some headline-seeking journalist nosing around here right now."

"Not to worry," I told her. "That's all been taken care of." And I then went on to explain the entire situation, including the fact that I'd told "Mrs. Wellington" that if she didn't leave Melissa alone I'd use the tape from the wildlife camera to expose her as the total fraud that she truly was.

"And so you think she's gone for good?" Melissa wondered.

"I know she's gone for good," I assured her. "In fact she was so very afraid that I'd ruin her career that she was practically groveling at the end."

"Well thank god for that," she said, greatly relieved. "There's just so very much that I have to lose."

"Because she might have found out about your grow room?" I assumed.

She paused for a moment or two, knitting her brow, and then gave me a rather reluctant look. "That's certainly a big part of it," she agreed, "but to tell you the truth it goes much deeper than just me growing a little medical marijuana."

"In what sense?"

And that's when I suddenly saw the most striking change in Melissa's demeaner. The seemingly strong and self-confident woman who'd worked so very hard to establish and nurture this incredibly beautiful botanical garden simply vanished. And in her place I saw someone highly vulnerable, her eyes revealing a certain degree of helplessness, or maybe even outright fear, as if her entire world was about to come crashing down around her.

And yet it wasn't all that long before she was somehow able to gather herself and slowly shake her head. "It's actually quite a long story," she then told me. "Are you sure that you want to hear the whole thing?"

"Absolutely," I replied. "And I say that mainly because I get the feeling that if you hold it in any longer it just might tear you apart."

She responded to that with a sardonic chuckle. "Am I really all that transparent?"

"Typically, no. But at the moment, yes."

"Well in that case," she said, her shoulders slumping a little, "please bear with me. This could very well take awhile."

And having said that she led me over to a little wrought iron bench that stood in front of a wellspring bubbling up out of moss-covered rocks, where as we sat down she silently collected her thoughts. "It all has to do with my Trust Fund," she eventually began, which came as such an enormous surprise that it was all I could do to keep from butting right in.

And Melissa must have sensed that, because she reached over and laid a hand on my knee. "Be patient," she told me. "As I said there's an awful lot to the story."

And drawing her hand back she then began anew. "Yes, that is indeed how I'm able to afford this garden. My parents were wealthy, very wealthy, although their money comes from a source that's so repulsive to me that I can barely even bring myself to tell you about it."

And almost as if to reinforce that point she had to pause to draw in a really deep breath. "Strip-mining," she then managed to say, although it was clearly very difficult for her to admit it. "In fact the largest strip-mining operation in the entire history of Appalachia. Over the years my father's company has leveled mountaintop after mountaintop to get at all of those precious deposits of coal, an inescapable reality that will never,

ever cease to haunt me. I mean even as a child I sensed that there was something wrong with the way that my family made its fortune, although I was far too young and naïve to understand what the business was really all about."

And with that she once again shook her head, and then gave me a very slight wistful smile. "And the irony is that it was ultimately being so very rich that led to my parent's death. They were flying off on a ski holiday in Montana when their private jet slid off an icy runway and crashed into a hangar. And just like that they were gone. I was only twenty-five at the time, and had just returned home from my stay on the Wind River reservation, so once the final legalities were completely settled and I had access to more money than I ever could have imagined I began to look for the perfect piece of property on which to build my very own little private sanctuary. And that's how I ended up here."

"Then what about your father's company? Is it still in business?"

Melissa gave me a rather slow and seemingly painful nod. "Yes, I'm really ashamed to say. And not only is it doing well, it's flat out thriving."

"But you don't actually have anything to do with running it yourself do you?"

"No. Not at all. But there's nothing I can do to stop the damage the company continues to do to the earth, and according to one of the conditions of my Trust I'm not even allowed to speak publicly about that damage. And that torments me every single day. In fact my only real solace comes from knowing that I'm using the company's profits to establish and maintain my garden, thereby replenishing the earth and spreading the word about the need to respect and care for Mother Nature as a whole. It's just about the only thing that really keeps me sane."

She broke off just long enough to look me straight in the eye. "So what really frightens me is the all too real possibility that I might someday lose Eternal Bloom. My Trust is overseen by a man named Jonathan Westerly, the lawyer who's now the head of my father's company, and he and I couldn't possibly be more at odds. He's all about Big Coal, and money, and power. And I'm all about doing whatever is necessary to protect the earth. So needless to say we haven't ever really gotten along. In fact he keeps a very close eye on everything that I do, hoping against hope that I might someday violate one of the conditions of my Trust, because he'd like nothing more than to be able to revoke that Trust and use the money to reinvest in the business."

"And just how very strict are these conditions?"

"It's not so much that they're so strict," she told me. "It's more that they're a constant threat hanging over my head, and keep me from expressing how I truly do feel. And Jonathon not only knows that, but he seems to take some sort of perverse pleasure in lording it over me, just waiting for me to make a mistake."

"Such as what?"

And boy was I surprised when Melissa then actually quoted from those conditions. "The beneficiary," she began in a voice heavy with emotion, "shall not denigrate or bring shame upon the family name, or family business, in any singular manner, including but not limited to public criticism or the commission of a felony."

"And that of course puts you in a rather awkward, if not downright precarious position."

"To put it mildly," she said with a really weak smile.

"So not only do you have to keep your opinions about strip-mining to yourself, but if you were ever busted for poaching plants, or growing pot, or any other felony offense, you'd ultimately lose your garden."

"And thereby aid in the growth of my father's company," she added.

And yet even though the thought of that clearly made her cringe, I could also tell by the underlying tone of her voice that she'd be willing to do just about anything she had to do to make sure that that never would happen.

⁂ ⁂ ⁂

I was up and out the door a little after nine the next morning, having agreed to meet Molly at Hopewell Lake to collect another round of algae samples. And it was such an unbelievably lovely day, the air soft and warm and the sky perfectly clear, that I decided to ride my bike instead of drive. So by the time I arrived to find Molly already there I was fully energized and ready to go.

And she certainly appeared to be all fired up too, having already laid her petri dishes out on a picnic table and stripped off her Fairfield hoodie in preparation of wading into the water.

"The algae's really bloomed since we were here the other day," she said as I approached. "So it should be pretty easy for us to get some really good samples."

And with that she suddenly fell silent and cocked her head, listening to a bird singing from out of the trees off to our left. "A cardinal," she then said, clearly delighted.

And much to my surprise she then pursed her lips and broke into a perfect imitation of the cardinal's song. Of course that alone would have been impressive enough, so you can well imagine how pleased I was when she actually received a melodic response, the two of them calling out back and forth, and back and forth, the cardinal obviously doing its best to establish some sort of dominance, its call getting louder and louder and more and more insistent.

Until Molly eventually broke off and said, "I just love doing that. The cardinal's by far my favorite bird."

"And you do a hell of a fine job of imitating it too."

"Well thank you," she said. "There are a few other bird calls I know as well, but that's easily the one I do best. And talking to any kind of bird at all never fails to lift my spirits."

And after punctuating that last claim with a bright and sunny smile, she then grabbed her share of the petri dishes and headed out across the beach, setting off a memory that hadn't occurred to me in years. After spending an entire day fighting my way through a steamy lowland jungle in Uruguay, I arrived at camp hot, tired, and filthy, my skin covered in a really nasty sheen of greasy sweat. So once I was settled in I immediately made a beeline to the deep wilderness river my team and I had chosen to spend the night beside.

Just as I was about to step off the shoreline, however, my native guide rushed over and grabbed me by the shoulder. "I do not think you want to go into that water," he said, his deep brown eyes searching mine in concern.

"Why not?" I wondered.

And that's when I learned a valuable lesson about not taking a foreign environment for granted. "Because," he said in as grave a voice as I'd ever heard, "by the time you are no more than three meters in, the piranha will have eaten all the flesh off your ankles."

So needless to say, I settled for very carefully filling a bucket with water and wiping myself down with a towel.

❧ ❧ ❧

Wanting to make the most of this beautiful day, I called Melissa and told her that I wouldn't be in until the next morning, and then I drove up to the lovely little county park about an hour north of Fairfield and went for a relatively easy six mile hike, mostly through gently rolling woodlands and open meadows full of tall grasses that waved back and forth in the wind. And even after I'd returned home I still wasn't quite ready to spend the entire evening inside, so I got in touch with Lily and invited her over for a bonfire.

"That's a really nice firepit," she said as I threw in a couple of more logs of wild cherry, hands down my favorite campfire wood because it burns so clean and smells so good.

"Thank you," I told her, using the toe of my boot to realign one of the large fieldstones I'd gathered from around my property and stacked three deep in a circle. "It was a lot of fun to build, although I have to admit that I really don't use it all that much."

"Then maybe you should date more," she said with a little laugh. "This is a seriously romantic setting, you know."

"More?" I responded with a sardonic chuckle. "I haven't been on a date in years."

"I can't imagine why not. There are certainly plenty of single women to be had around here."

"Oh, I don't know," I said. "When I was traveling so much I just didn't think it would be fair to subject anyone to my lifestyle, since my schedule was often so spontaneous and I was normally away for so long. Not to mention my lack of a steady income at the time. I mean I was depending solely on grants and private donations to support myself, and what kind of a life would that be for a woman?"

"Then what about now? You've been here in Ohio for nearly a year, and on a college campus teeming with available young women too. I'd think that at the very least you'd have been tempted to ask somebody out."

"I'm sure I will be one of these days," I told her, setting about poking the coals with a stick because I easily get tired of talking about myself.

And as a flurry of sparks suddenly rose up into the sky I then turned the conversation back around to Lily. "So what about you? I don't recall you dating much either."

She gave me a rather incredulous look, the firelight illuminating her cheekbones. "Are you kidding? I only recently got my youngest out of the house, you know, and can't even begin to tell you how much I'm enjoying the peace and quiet of being alone. So the last thing I need right now's somebody new coming into my life. Besides"—and she stared deep into the fire for a heartbeat or two—"having already been through a failed marriage I have to confess to being a little leery about relationships in general."

"That only makes sense," I said. "And at the risk of maybe getting just a little too personal, what was it that happened there?"

She thought back, carefully weighing her response, and then very slowly smiled to herself. "Oh nothing really happened, I guess. There wasn't any real drama, or anything like that. Things just weren't working out anymore. The love was simply no longer there."

And having said that she slowly shook her head, and then went right back to staring into the fire. And since I was completely at a loss as to what to say myself, I simply set about staring into the fire as well, the only sound the crackling and popping of the burning wood. It certainly wasn't an awkward silence though. Just a quiet communion among really good friends.

❧ ❧ ❧

After all of the drama surrounding the commercial nursery owner and "Mrs. Wellington," the next person Melissa drew my attention to came as a bit of a relief. I was busy classifying a series of conifers at the back of the garden when she came walking along a flagstone path with a young lady dressed in what I guess I'd have to call funky casual workwear, a trendy navy tunic over a pair of khaki slacks.

"Devin," she said once they'd reached me, "this is Wendy Wilhelm. She with an organization called Eliminate Hunger Now, and she came in to discuss something I know very little about. But since I'm assuming that you probably do, I thought maybe you could help to fill me in."

"I'd certainly be happy to give it a try," I told her. And turning to Miss Wilhelm I extended my hand. "Devin Douglass," I said.

"Nice to meet you, Dr. Douglass," she replied, giving my hand a gentle squeeze. "I'm familiar with some of your work."

"Really?"

"Yes, but not so much your academic writing as your reputation as a botanist in the field."

"Well I must say that I'm flattered," I told her. And because her Twiggy-like pixie haircut and youthful green eyes made her look like she couldn't possibly be older than maybe her mid-twenties I couldn't keep from adding, "But I'm also a little surprised. You just don't strike me as someone who'd have a whole lot of experience along those lines."

"To be honest," she said with a self-deprecating smile, "I don't. But I completed my Ph.D. in Botany at Ohio State just last year, so of course with Fairfield being so close by I heard all about you coming there to teach. After all, your arrival created quite a buzz around here, you know."

"So they tell me," I confessed, "although I must say that I don't pay too much attention to any of that. All it does is distract me from what's really important."

And with that I got back to the point. "So what is it that you've come here to talk about?"

"Advanced photosynthesis," she was quick to say. "That was the primary topic of my dissertation, and I'm absolutely convinced that it lies at the heart of the future of food production."

"That's very interesting," I said with a thoughtful nod. And then, to Melissa, "And I suppose that's what you'd like me to help Wendy explain to you?"

"That's it all right. I'm familiar with the basics of photosynthesis of course, but that's about it."

"Well given your love of plants, I think that you're going to enjoy what Wendy and I have to say. And on that note, would you like to start, Wendy, or would you like me to?"

"You go right on ahead," she said, "and I'll jump in whenever I can."

"Okay then. Here we go. During photosynthesis plants use sunlight, carbon dioxide, and water to create carbohydrates as food to fuel their growth, with the only real byproduct being oxygen, which of course we need in abundance simply to survive."

And breaking off I said to Wendy, "How am I doing so far?"

"Just fine," she said with an encouraging smile.

"Then would you like to take over for now?"

"Sure," she replied, her face lighting up. "And advanced photosynthesis is the process of enhancing what plants naturally do on their own, thereby providing stronger, healthier, disease and pest resistant plants that mature much faster than the standard growth rate, which would definitely help to feed an ever larger world population through increased crop yields while at the same time allowing farmers to cut down on their use of harmful chemical fertilizers and pesticides."

And boy did that explanation make a big impression on me, although it wasn't Wendy's beautifully detailed overview itself that I found to be so very compelling. It was more the amazing amount of enthusiasm with which she expressed it. I mean, she was so incredibly excited by the potential impact of advanced photosynthesis that she was practically radiating a youthful idealism.

And from Melissa's wide-eyed reaction, I could tell that she found Wendy's nearly poetic explanation to be deeply touching as well. Unfortunately that caused me a great deal of concern, and I knew right then and there that she and I would most definitely have to discuss the matter in private. If not she could very well be in for one hell of a lot of trouble.

❧ ❧ ❧

"What an engaging young lady," Melissa said as we watched Wendy driving off down the dogwood-lined lane. "She even reminds me a little of myself at that age. You know, just starting out with little more than big dreams and a whole lot of positive energy, bound and determined to make her mark on the world."

"And that kind of gives you hope for the future, doesn't it?"

"I'll say it does. So much so, in fact, that it makes me feel as if I should try to do something to help her."

And that's exactly what I was afraid of. "In what way?" I asked.

"Oh, I don't know," she said with a sigh. "It just seems like I ought to be able to do something. After all, I've dedicated my entire life to growing plants, you know."

"Then do you mind if I offer you a word of advice?"

"Not at all," she said as if she didn't know why I even bothered to ask. "You've done so much for me already that I'd be a fool not to listen to whatever you have to say."

"Well thank you," I told her. "I do what I can. I mean, it's pretty obvious that in many ways you and I are kindred spirits, so the very least we can do is support one another."

"Amen," she said with an acknowledging nod.

"And with that in mind," I then went on, "I'm afraid that I have to express a rather serious reservation."

And having made that point I was very careful about how I worded what I had to say next, because I wasn't quite ready to let Melissa know that I'd gone to the extreme of spying on her in the solarium the other day. "From what I can tell from the time I've spent working here," I began, "it appears to me that you close your garden down during the noon hour because that's when you really concentrate on healing the sick plants in your care."

I paused for a moment to see how she'd react to that, but she merely gave me a somewhat passive look, as if curious but a little leery to hear whatever else I might have to say in that regard. So I simply forged on ahead. "And there are two very good reasons why I think that, Melissa. One, it only makes sense that you'd draw upon the power of the sun to facilitate the healing process, so what better time to make use of it than when it's at its strongest? And two, it's almost painfully clear to me that healing those plants really takes a hell of a lot out of you. I mean whenever I see you in the early afternoon you're visibly tired, run down, worn out. In other words you're giving so much of yourself to the healing process that it's draining you of an unhealthy amount of your own energy. Are you aware of that at all?"

"More than you could ever know," she said in a voice so weary as to leave no doubt.

"Then if you barely have enough strength to heal a few house plants on a daily basis, what makes you think you'd have anything to offer Wendy on a much, much larger scale?"

She hung her head for a moment, taking that to heart, and then looked back up and softly said, "But it's such an incredibly worthy cause that I'd feel really bad if I didn't reach out to her somehow."

"And you know what?" I told her. "I definitely think you should reach out to her too. Just not by sacrificing yourself physically. You simply don't have the strength."

"Then what did you have in mind?" she wondered, sounding just a little bit testy.

"A couple of things, actually," I told her. "Depending on the size of your Trust Fund, you could offer Wendy a generous donation. Organizations like hers can always use the money, you know. And beyond that you could help to publicize her cause by printing up brochures to hand out to all of the people who tour your garden. Now I know that may not sound like a whole hell of a lot, but at least you'd be making an effort. And I'm sure that Wendy would appreciate that."

She considered those possibilities for a moment, her eyes taking on kind of a far away look. And then she gave a little shrug as if to say why not. "All right then. That's exactly what I'll do. And in the meantime I'll see if maybe I can come up with a few other ways to help her as well."

"That's the spirit," I told her. "Everybody wins. Just be sure to keep your own well-being in mind."

"Oh, you don't have to worry about that," she told me. "I don't really have any other choice when it comes to managing my health."

And before I could even ask her what she meant by

that, she gave me kind of a bitter smile and then turned and walked away.

❦ ❦ ❦

After leaving Melissa's at eleven o'clock that morning, I drove south along the river to Big Walnut State Park, where I pulled in, got out of my car, and removed my hybrid bike from the little trailer I was hauling. Then I rode on back up to Eternal Bloom, stashed my bike in among some holly bushes, and made my way over to the solarium. It was just after noon by then, and I was anxious to once again bear witness to Melissa healing plants. Or more accurately, I wanted to make sure that what I'd seen on my first undercover mission hadn't merely been a figment of my frequently overactive imagination.

And I'm extremely pleased to be able to report that the magical scene I came upon left no doubt whatsoever. I hadn't even reached the perimeter of the field in which the solarium stood when I saw a faint but undeniable light streaming through the trees. And the closer I got the brighter that light became... until I arrived at the edge of the clearing to find the entire solarium aglow with a golden radiance that emitted from within. It was such a powerful sight, in fact, that it was all I could do to force myself to eventually turn away, my entire being so full of a sense of wonder that it left me in total awe.

❦ ❦ ❦

I was in my office doing a little reading later on that day when Molly paid me an unexpected visit, looking very much like a starry-eyed young hippie in what I liked to refer to as an "earth mother" dress, a loose-fitting cotton shift with flowers embroidered across the chest and all the way down the sleeves. It stood out in stark contrast to the somber look on her face.

"I hope I'm not bothering you," she said as she took her usual seat across from me. "But I was analyzing algae samples in the conservatory a little while ago when Dr. Watson came in, and we had a conversation that I think you need to know about."

Needless to say that piqued my interest. "And..." I prompted.

She absent-mindedly pushed a lock of frizzy red hair behind one ear. "And he kind of creeped me out," she said, "because he kept asking me stuff that made me really uncomfortable."

I scooted up onto the edge of my seat. "Such as what?"

"Well first of all he wanted me to know that he'd learned about the two of us working together out at Hopewell Lake, and then he kind of started pressing me for details about our relationship."

And all I could think of was oh Jesus, that asshole. Are there no limits as to how low he's willing to go? "And so what did you tell him?"

"I told him the truth, that there really is no relationship. At least not personally. We were just out there doing research in the field. He didn't seem at all satisfied with that answer, though, and kept pushing me on the issue. It was like he was trying real hard to dig up a little dirt on you or something, so I thought I'd better come over here and let you know about it."

"Well you've done just the right thing," I assured her. "Thank you. I'm just sorry that you had to be subjected to all of this. Academia can get downright nasty at times, and this is just one of those occasional unfortunate situations. And yet the fact that he'd drag you into it really crosses the line as to what's acceptable, so you can leave it to me to deal with him from here on out. And believe me I'll take care of it."

"So I'm not in any trouble?" she said, and I could tell by the tone of her voice that she was worried about negating all the progress she'd made at school over the past few months.

"No, you're not in any trouble at all. You haven't done anything wrong. And I'll make sure that this doesn't keep you from completing your research. You've got a great project going, Molly, and I really want you to be able to see it all the way through. And with me helping you out whenever you need me too."

That clearly came as a big relief, so much so, in fact, that as I was gently ushering Molly out of my office she once again gave me a spontaneous hug.

While busy classifying a row of neatly pruned shrubs the next morning I thought of something I wanted to talk to Melissa about, and since she told me that she'd be in her potting shed if I needed her, I walked over there and found that she was down in her grow room.

"I'll be up in a minute," she yelled when I let her know I was there, the rich scent of her marijuana plants filling the air.

So I took the opportunity to get a better feel for the place, and was particularly attracted to an antique oak cabinet that had a handwritten sign on the front that said Medicinals. It was chock full of little bottles, and jars, and vials of dried plants, and oils, and dews she'd collected, each one clearly labeled as to both its contents and the various ailments it could help to relieve. And that, of course, gave me a whole new level of respect for the incredibly intimate relationship Melissa had developed with the natural world.

And that's when she came climbing up the stairs from her secret room, lowering the trap door and sliding the throw rug back into place. Her hands were dirty and there was a water stain on her overalls, so my guess was that she must have been repotting plants.

"I've been down there all morning and could really use some fresh air," she told me, wiping her hands on a towel she'd picked up off a stool. "So if you need to talk why don't we go outside?"

And with that she led me out the door and down a brick-lined path to a screened-in gazebo that stood among young apple trees next to the river. I'd passed by it any number of times before, but had never yet been inside.

"This is where I often sleep on hot summer nights," she told me as we stepped in, "all the better to breath the moist night air and feel the cool breeze coming in off the water."

"It's lovely," I told her as I took note of the wood-framed canvas cot, maple nightstand, and battery-powered lantern. Then we both sat down on the bench that lined the inner perimeter and Melissa turned to me and said, "So, what's on your mind?"

"Oh nothing terribly important. I just wanted to ask you about a term that kept coming up in a book I was reading yesterday afternoon."

"Well then, go right ahead and I'll tell you whatever I can."

"Thanks," I said. "Ever since you let me know about the time you spent studying under an Arapaho Medicine Woman I've been looking into the relationship between Native Americans and nature, and what I was reading yesterday kept referring to something I'm not familiar with. It's called 'The Honorable Harvest.'"

Her eyes lit up in a way that I never would've imagined. It was almost as if I'd touched a nerve, so to speak. And yet it wasn't a physical nerve. It was something deep in her soul. "You first have to realize," she then said in a solemn voice, "that this isn't a concept to be taken lightly. In fact it lies at the very heart of my hope for the future of mankind."

And I have to admit that I wasn't expecting anything nearly that dramatic. Nonetheless, I was able to gather myself and give her a nod to show that I understood. And after staring at me just long enough to make sure that I truly did appreciate the gravity of the matter, she then leaned back up against the wall of the gazebo, collected her thoughts, and began to speak about an age-old way of life that would forever change the manner in which I viewed this world.

"The Honorable Harvest," she began, "is the philosophy behind the Native American's approach to maintaining the health of the earth, and it is so far-reaching and nuanced that I couldn't even begin to do it justice in one brief sitting. So I'll simply give you a couple of key principles and leave it at that. If you'd like to know more you'll have to go ahead and do the research on your own."

"I'd be more than happy to listen to whatever you're willing to tell me," I said.

"Very well then, principle number one: Take only what you need. The earth is here to provide us with all of the natural resources we depend on to sustain our lives, and as long as we take only what we need it will continue to provide those resources until the ultimate end of time. Taking too much, however, depletes the earth, and throws the entire cycle of life completely out of balance."

She paused for a moment to gauge my reaction, and must have seen that I was suitably impressed, because she almost immediately began talking again. "And principle number two: Take only what is given to you, which to me personally applies mostly to our energy needs. After all, the sun will always continue to shine. The wind will always continue to blow. And the tides will always continue to roll up onto the shore. Thus providing us with all of the energy we need without doing any damage to the earth whatsoever."

She paused again, this time to lower her head and stare down into her lap. And a moment later, when she looked back up, her face was pale and her voice was so strained that she could barely even get the words out. "But by no stretch of the imagination is a fossil fuel like coal freely given to us. We have no choice but to wound the land, and foul the water and air, to forcefully gouge it from the earth. And then there are the lasting repercussions of actually being foolish enough to burn it, thereby releasing millions of years of safely stored carbons right back up into the atmosphere."

And that's when she broke off for good. Not because she didn't have anything more to say. That much was obvious to me. But because pursuing that particular line of thought was much too painful for her to bear. Or to put it more simply, she was completely overwhelmed by guilt.

❧ ❧ ❧

I was following Melissa off the front steps of the gazebo when she somehow caught her foot and began to stumble, but luckily I was able to reach out and grab her by the arm before she went all the way down. And yet rather than thanking me she actually became more than a little upset.

"I'm fine," she said once she'd regained her balance, abruptly yanking her arm out of my grasp.

And because that was so very much out of character I got the feeling that there was something more going on here than was readily apparent. It's just that I didn't have even the slightest idea as to what that something could possibly be. Still, there was no mistaking the sudden anger that had come over her, so I knew that I definitely had to keep an eye out for any future signs of exactly what it was that might be troubling her.

❧ ❧ ❧

"Looks like it might rain," Lily said as we strolled along the hike and bike trail that ran not too far from my little bungalow.

And gazing up at the dark clouds rolling in from the west, I had no choice but to agree. "Still, I don't see any thunderheads, or anything really severe. So I'm guessing we'll be okay. Besides, after spending twenty-eight straight days in a steady downpour in the rain forests of Papa New Guinea a couple of years ago, I can't imagine that a few sprinkles are going to be all that difficult to deal with anyway."

"So do you miss it?" she said, and then caught herself and giggled. "I mean not the rain, but all that adventure? You know, always going new places and doing new things?"

"Oh, not really. Eight years of almost constantly battling adverse conditions were more than enough for me. So right now I'm perfectly happy with the creature comforts of a fairly normal existence."

"In spite of all the crap that you have to put up with at Fairfield, right?"

I glanced over at her and pretended to scowl. "You would have to bring that up, wouldn't you?"

"Sorry," she said, giving me a somewhat of an embarrassed smile. "It's just that ever since William Watson tried to intimidate me it's pretty much been on my mind."

"Well you know what's been good for me along those lines?"

"No," she said with a shake of her head, clearly curious about what that might be.

"Working out at Eternal Bloom. It's just such an idyllic environment that it's kind of hard to get upset about anything while I'm there. Although having just said that, I do have to admit to being somewhat concerned about Melissa."

"And why's that?" Lily asked.

"It's actually kind of hard to say. I mean there's not any one thing that really stands out. It's more like there's a whole bunch of little things that make me think that something about her's just not quite right."

"Such as what, for example?"

And that's when I first felt a drop of rain. So I suggested that we should probably turn around, and once we did I went on to say, "Well, for one thing I see her hands trembling every now and again. And she also seems a little clumsy, and a little spacy at times, almost as if she's struggling just to put her thoughts together."

"Wow," Lily said. "Those could be signs of a lot of different things. Stress. Low blood sugar. Diabetes. Even a serious neurological problem."

And no sooner had she said that than my thoughts flashed back to when Melissa had told me that she'd first started growing marijuana to help her aunt deal with the symptoms of Parkinson's Disease. And for just a second there I couldn't help but wonder if perhaps there was more to that story than she'd been willing to let on. I didn't know why that had suddenly occurred to me, but it sure as hell had. And since over the years my intuitions had almost always pointed me in the right direction, I decided that it would probably be in my best interest to make an effort to find out what it was that I now suspected she'd been keeping from me all along.

※ ※ ※

"So what do you think?" Melissa asked as we sat on the front steps of her storybook Tudor cottage.

And handing back the shiny new brochure she'd just given me to look over, I told her that I thought she'd done a really good job. "Not only do you present a terrific overview of Wendy's organization, but I particularly like the heart-warming personal stories of the individuals and communities they've already been able to help overcome hunger."

"But will it motivate people to donate?"

"I don't see why not, especially since you've put so much emphasis on Eternal Bloom being a major sponsor. I mean the type of people who really like your garden would most definitely fit the profile of those who'd also been willing to contribute to making sure that the less fortunate don't go without food. Or at least that's what it seems like to me."

"That's what I was hoping you'd say," she told me. And then, with a look so sly as to kind of catch me off guard, "And just so you don't worry about me overextending myself physically, I want you to know that I've also come up with another way to help Wendy that won't directly involve me at all."

"Seriously?" I said, really pleased to hear that.

"Yep. I've been talking with a young man who showed up the other day wanting to know more about my ability to heal sick plants. But unlike most of the others who've recently come by hoping to learn more about me, he's not looking to profit from my abilities. Quite the opposite in fact. He's clearly an idealist who's dedicated himself to changing the world for the better, and in a way that's really dear to my heart too."

I stared out at a robin that was splashing around in a beautifully sculpted bird bath across the way. "Then my guess is that it must have something to do with meeting our energy needs."

"Exactly," she said. "He's fascinated by my ability to regenerate plants because he's working on finding the most effective way to produce plant-based solar fuels, and since that no doubt has to involve the process of photosynthesis then who better to put him in touch with than Wendy? I mean think about it. The two of them would not only be able to help one another, but the results could very well benefit nearly everybody on the planet. And the only role I'd have to play would be that of the matchmaker, so to speak. Does that sound like a really good idea or what?"

It sounded like a really good idea indeed, and that's exactly what I told Melissa, who then gave me a little self-satisfied grin and began to radiate a subtle but unmistakable glow. It was by far the healthiest I'd seen her look over the few weeks since we'd first met.

6

"I'm having even more trouble with Dr. Watson," Molly O'Grady confessed as she sat across from me during our normal weekly conference.

And that caused me to feel just a little bit guilty, because even though I'd scheduled a meeting with Henry Chandler to discuss the problems I'd been having with William Watson, it hadn't yet taken place. So to my way of thinking I'd let her down. "And what's going on now?" I asked her.

"Oh it's just more of that same old creepy stuff," she told me. "He cornered me in the conservatory again this morning, and started talking about how one of his colleagues had seen me giving you a hug. Then he asked me if maybe I was just thanking you for the stipend I'd recently been awarded. And when I said yes, he kind of leaned in and rubbed up against me, saying that he had access to quite a bit of grant money that might be of interest to me."

She broke off at that point, visibly shaken, and then bent over to reach into her beaded macramé shoulder bag, drawing out a tissue and wiping her eyes. "The thing is," she then went on, "I'm pretty sure that I know how to keep him away from me. It's just that I'm a nobody here at Fairfield, and he's a really powerful person, so I'm kind of afraid to take the risk."

"The risk of doing what?" I asked.

And in response she reached down into her shoulder bag again, coming out with the little recorder she used to collect bird calls and setting it on my desk. "Well when I saw him coming my way this morning I assumed the worst, so I quickly stuck my hand in my shoulder bag and turned this on. The sound quality's actually pretty good too. I've got every last word that he said."

"Well I'll be damned," I muttered to myself, thinking that between that tape and my analysis of Watson's vengeful but shabby academic writing, I now had all the ammunition I needed to try to convince Henry Chandler to put a lot of pressure on him to leave me the hell alone.

"Molly," I then said with a grateful smile, "you are an absolute godsend."

And even though she reacted to that compliment with a look of total confusion, I could tell that she was really happy to know that I actually thought so highly of her.

❧ ❧ ❧

I sat at the base of the now towering and glorious sugar maple that my grandfather had planted behind Rutherford Hall when he first came to Fairfield in the early 1900's, deriving a great deal of comfort from its sheltering boughs and the familiar feel of its rough bark against my back. I often came there when I was troubled, or conflicted, or maybe even just needed a little peace and quiet—which is exactly what I was looking for at that very moment. Given everything that had taken place over the past few weeks, I just felt as if I could use a bit of down time to organize my thoughts, put it all into perspective, and gather the strength I knew I'd need to both deal with William Watson and solve the many mysteries surrounding Melissa Davis, not to mention her magical, dare I even say supernatural ability to heal sick plants.

It was a lovely time of day to be sitting there too, the sun having just now fully cleared the horizon and the campus green so quiet and still that it was almost as if the day was practically trembling with the desire to get underway. I mean there was so much latent energy in the air that the entire world seemed to consist of nothing but untapped potential. And as I drew in and released a really deep breath, I somehow knew that if I simply set my mind to the matters at hand, and continued ever forward with a heart forever pure, then no matter what challenges the next few days might bring, everything would eventually work out just fine.

❧ ❧ ❧

Henry Chandler clicked off Molly O'Grady's little recorder and set it on top of The American Journal of Botany he'd been reading just a few minutes before. Then he reached into the breast pocket of his tweed suitcoat and drew out his burnished leather smoking pouch. Unfolding it, he removed his well-seasoned meerschaum pipe and began to pack it with the specialized three-tobacco blend he'd long been so very fond of. And only then did he finally speak.

"I can offer my full assurance," he said, "that Dr. Watson will no longer be of any concern to either you or Miss O'Grady. Given his stature here at Fairfield, as well as the fact that he's long been tenured, I hesitate to file a formal grievance against him. But I will indeed give him a stern lecture about the need to behave in a more ethical manner, and I will warn him that if he ever again oversteps his bounds in even the slightest of ways... he will then be summarily dismissed. I trust that meets with your expectations."

"As long as he leaves Molly and me alone," I told him, thinking that he conveniently forgot to mention the vast amounts of grant money that William Watson brought in, "I really don't give a damn what happens to him."

Henry leaned back in his chair, his rather prodigious belly straining against the fabric of his vest. "That's very diplomatic of you, my boy, and given the need to maintain a certain degree of stability within our department, a very unselfish stance to take as well. I should think that your grandfather would have been pleased."

And with that he reached up to push his bifocals a little further back up onto the bridge of his distinctly bulbous nose, his face so blank that I had to assume that our meeting was now officially over. Just as I was getting ready to leave, however, he quietly cleared his throat and said, "Oh, and by the way, the dean recently informed me that due to an exceptional fund-raising season we now have the money to create a new undergraduate scholarship, and I can think of no better qualified candidate than your Miss O'Grady. Do you think that she would possibly have any interest in accepting such an offer?"

And as I thought about Molly's struggle with her self-image during her first year and a half here at Fairfield, and the enormous amount of confidence she'd gained in just these past few months, all I could do was smile and nod.

❧ ❧ ❧

Melissa eased down next to me on a swing that hung from an oak bough along the bank of the Seneca River, the early afternoon sun glistening off the ripples in the gently flowing water. "This is such a beautiful place," she then said in a rather wistful and yet slightly weary voice, which seemed perfectly fitting considering that she'd just now made her way down from the solarium, and her daily healing session.

And it was then that I noticed the fingers on her left hand trembling just a little, and thanks to my recent conversation with Lily I now had a pretty good idea as to what that could possibly mean. "So I've been wondering... " I said, turning to look at her so that I could gauge her reaction.

"About what?" she asked.

"Oh, a lot of different things really. This garden. Your grow room. Your poor old aunt who has Parkinson's. You never really have told me very much about her."

She remained silent for a moment, eyeing me suspiciously. "And exactly what is it that you'd like to know?"

"Nothing really all that important. Just, you know, whether or not you guys are close. And how she's doing. Stuff like that. After all, you're taking a huge risk to help her fight her disease, so I'd have to think that she must be on your mind a lot."

She continued to study me for just another moment. "It's actually a rather private matter," she then said dismissively.

And it was so incredibly unusual for her to be that defensive that I instantly knew that I must have been on to something. So I immediately cut to the quick. "She doesn't even really exist, does she?"

And in response her entire body stiffened and she looked at me defiantly, but only until I gently reached over and lay a reassuring hand on her forearm. That's when all of the fight went out of her and she slowly lowered her head, staring despondently down into her lap, where both of her hands were now trembling lightly.

So I gave her a few seconds to compose herself before quietly asking, "And how long has it been since you were first diagnosed?"

And once again her only reply was a rather lengthy silence, the river lapping rhythmically upon the shore, and the leaves rustling softly in the cool spring breeze. Until, "It's been just a little over two years now."

"And how have you been holding up so far?"

She gazed aimlessly out over the water before giving me an answer, and I could tell by how relaxed her body had become that she was actually kind of relieved that the truth was now finally out. "Oh, about as well as could be expected, I suppose. Although some days are definitely better than others, and the bad ones seem to come around a lot more frequently now. So who's to say what's going to happen from here."

"Then what about your garden? I mean if your disease does indeed continue to progress, then what's going to happen to it?"

And all she could do was shake her head. "I don't know," she said in a voice heavy with despair. "I honestly do not know."

And without another word she immediately returned to gazing out over the water, clearly struggling, not only with the fact that her body had betrayed her, but also with the threat her diminishing abilities posed to the botanical paradise that over the years had become the very center of her world.

꧁ ꧂ ꧃

"So something just occurred to me," I said to Melissa as we were walking back up towards her cottage. "I only have a year left on my appointment at Fairfield, and all things considered I've found that I'm really not at all that happy with my life in academia. There's just too much bureaucratic bullshit to put up with, not to mention the unbelievable interpersonal hassles, what with all of the political infighting and backbiting and the rest of that totally unnecessary but unavoidable crap."

At that point a heavily spotted fawn suddenly appeared on the path up ahead, stopping to look at us for just a brief moment before bounding off into the trees. "And because of all that," I then continued, "I wouldn't really have anything against maybe looking for another line of work. Something, you know, less structured and more suited to my love of actually being out in nature."

And that's when Melissa turned her face my way and we both gradually came to a stop. "Like maybe looking after a botanical garden?" she said, a sudden glint of hope in her eye. "Is that what you're trying to tell me?"

"Something like that," I admitted.

"It's an awful lot of work," she continued. "Probably more than you realize."

"That doesn't bother me in the slightest," I told her, "not considering the type of work that we're talking about. And anyway, if worse came to worse I have a really close colleague I'm pretty damn sure I could talk into coming to work right alongside me."

"Seriously?"

"Yep. And I'm absolutely certain that you'd really like her too. She may not be quite as attuned to the natural world as you are, but believe me she's perfectly capable nonetheless."

"Well then what about the particulars? You know, the pay scale? The hours? Practical matters such as that."

"Something tells me we'll be able to work that out. And once we do, that'll free you up to continue healing plants without having to worry about the rest of your garden."

"You know" she said in as light a voice as I'd heard her speak in all day, "I'm guessing you might actually have something there."

I gave her a slow and thoughtful nod. "Then as long as we're talking about how to relieve some of the pressure you're under, I have a couple of other ideas as well."

"Such as what?" she asked as if maybe that was just a little too good to be true.

"Well first of all," I said, "I am recognized as somewhat of a leader in the newly emerging field of psychoactive plants, you know."

"I am indeed well aware of that," she told me. "In fact if I recall it was somewhat of a controversial point when you were first hired on at Fairfield."

"That's putting it mildly," I admitted. "But right now it could very well work in your favor."

She gave me a rather doubtful look. "It's nice to hear you say that, but I certainly don't see how."

And that brought a big old smile to my face. "Well what I was thinking..." I said, letting my voice trail off just to build a little suspense.

"Go on," she urged, "and I'll try to keep an open mind."

"That shouldn't be too terribly hard to do," I told her. "In fact I think you're really going to like to hear what I have to say."

"In that case come on out with it," she said with just a hint of impatience.

So that's exactly what I did. "Well due to the fact that

the drug culture has become so predominant over this past decade, the government's been encouraging research projects in an effort to get a grip on what in the hell's going on. So it should be pretty easy for me to apply for a grant that would enable the two of us to grow marijuana legally. Say, for example, because we want to study its medicinal use in fighting Parkinson's Disease. I mean while I was out traveling the world to discover new plants I applied for and received any number of government grants, so I've already established a whole lot of contacts in that regard. And if you don't mind me saying so, I've also established a pretty solid reputation for turning out great results too. And therefore a government funded project such as the one I just mentioned should actually be a no-brainer."

She gazed at me quietly as she considered that fact, a light mist rising up in her eyes. "I can't even begin to tell you how much that would mean to me," she then said.

"And along those same lines," I told her, "I also have a lot of experience raising money from private benefactors too. In fact you'd be surprised at how many wealthy nature-lovers there are who'd be more than happy to contribute to projects that would help to guarantee the well-being of our precious Mother Earth. So if by some odd chance you happened to violate one of the conditions of your Trust and lost all of that income, I'm pretty damn sure that between the government funding and private donations I'd still be able to keep your garden up and running for... well, pretty much forever."

And that hit her with so much emotional force that for a brief second there I was afraid that her knees might actually buckle. But then she drew in a deep breath to steady herself and reached over to take me by the hand. "You sir," she said, giving my hand a light squeeze, "are an absolute blessing. I just wish that there was something I could do to show you how incredibly grateful I am."

"No problem there," I told her with a really sly grin. "In fact I know exactly what I'd like you to do."

She gave me somewhat of a quizzical look. "And what pray tell would that be?"

"Well, over these past few weeks I've come to know just about every single part of your garden, except of course for the inside of your solarium. So I'd really love for you to take me on in there."

"In that case," she said, immediately setting off down the path again, her voice drifting back over her shoulder, "please just follow me."

❧ ❧ ❧

Melissa and I took a seat in the very center of a tightly woven bamboo mat, surrounded by a dozen or so common houseplants in various stages of health, the air moist and warm and filled with the soft and soothing sound of a Native American flute. And yet what easily made the biggest impression on me was the enormous amount of energy that was building up around us. It was just so very much like what I'd experienced while sitting up against my grandfather's sugar maple that morning that the coincidence was downright eerie. I'd entered first and could immediately feel it, a heightened sense of anticipation, something wonderful getting ready to happen, the promise of a dream that was about to come true.

But it wasn't until Melissa entered right behind me that the level of that energy truly ramped up, a nearly palpable surge of hope and expectation, every last one of the plants actually leaning a little in her direction, exactly as they would while seeking out the life-giving light streaming down from the sky.

"So what do you think of the place?" Melissa asked

once we were completely settled, the entire interior taking on a subtle glow.

"It's simply amazing," I told her. "In fact I'm not even really sure how to describe it. It's just so full of... of... I don't know. An elemental power of some sort I suppose. I might even go so far as to say the very energy of the lifeforce itself."

"And that's exactly what it is," she said. "For sunlight's the source of all life as we know it. Any true visionary would tell you that."

"But how do you do it? I mean, how do you draw that energy down and pass it on to the plants?"

And boy was I surprised when she responded with a simple shrug. "I'm not really all that sure. Just lucky I guess. My belief is that everyone has their very own special gift. It's just that not too many of us ever truly realize that. And my gift just happens to be an unusually acute sensitivity to plants, which allows me to both intuit their needs and respond to whatever it is they may be. Thereby giving me the ability, not only to nurture them, but to heal them as well. Of course I never even would have known that if it wasn't for my Arapaho teacher and spiritual guide, who helped me to discover that gift by using methods that I'm afraid I'm not at liberty to discuss."

And thanks to my work with various native shaman deep in the jungles of Central America I understood that last point completely. "Well regardless of how you relate to your plants, the results are absolutely astounding."

And as she acknowledged that comment with a gracious little bow, I suddenly thought about how fortunate I now felt, because getting to know Melissa, and witnessing firsthand her seemingly mystical, or should I even say miraculous abilities had a truly profound effect on me. For it reinforced my long held belief in the enigmatic and yet undeniable accomplishments of my two botanical heroes, Luther Burbank and George Washington Carver, both of whom were able to do revolutionary work that not only totally confounded the scientific experts of their day, but will probably never ever be fully explained. And to me that merely underscored the true beauty of this wonderful and yet incredibly mysterious life. I mean the very fact that we even exist is by far the greatest miracle of all.

"So then," Melissa said at that point, struggling just a little to get to her feet and then waiting for me to stand up as well. "If you're eventually going to take over my garden, then we might as well get started right now. Let's head on over to my potting shed and I'll show you the secret ingredients for my specialized soil and mineral mix."

And even though it was all I could do just to tear myself away from the light that was now radiating throughout the solarium, I somehow knew deep down inside that I really had no other choice, for only by always taking advantage of the rare opportunities that came my way could I truly hope to fully ensure that there would forever be plenty of other enlightening adventures awaiting me somewhere on down the line.

END

Also by James Lake

Fiction

LETTING IN LIGHT
August, 2021

BAGMAN
January, 2019

HEAVEN SENT
January, 2016

A BOOMER IN THE BUD
December 2013

THE SOPHIA DIARY
April 2011

THE BIG BANG
AuthorHouse, March, 2007

James Lake

James Lake spent his entire career teaching at Kent State University, where he developed the belief that storytelling is crucial to both the preservation of the natural world and the growth of the human spirit.

His novels include THE BIG BANG, THE SOPHIA DIARY, A BOOMER IN THE BUD, HEAVEN SENT, BAGMAN, and LETTING IN LIGHT.